(continued)

Berkley Books by Sherwood Kiraly

DIMINISHED CAPACITY
BIG BABIES

DIMINISHED CAPACITY

SHERWOOD KIRALY

BERKLEY BOOKS, NEW YORK

DIMINISHED CAPACITY

A Berkley Book / published by arrangement with the author

PRINTING HISTORY
Berkley trade paperback edition / September 1995
Berkley mass market edition / May 1997

The Putnam Berkley World Wide Web site address is
http://www.berkley.com

ISBN: 0-425-15763-6

BERKLEY®
Berkley Books are published by The Berkley Publishing Group, 200 Madison Avenue, New York, New York 10016.
BERKLEY and the "B" design
are trademarks belonging to Berkley Publishing Corporation.

PRINTED IN THE UNITED STATES OF AMERICA

10 9 8 7 6 5 4 3 2 1

DIMINISHED
CAPACITY

Sherwood Kiraly

CHAPTER ONE

My uncle Roland Zerbs lives in LaPorte, Missouri, where I grew up. He's known locally as the Fish Man.

LaPorte is small, under a thousand population—too small for Uncle Rollie, who is a sufficient character for a much larger town. He's old now and no longer runs the basement tavern on Front Street, but he pursues his great hobby or obsession with even more intensity than he did when I was a little boy, thirty years ago.

It's always been Uncle Rollie's goal to publish the poetry written by the fish that live in the Mississippi River, which runs past LaPorte. And the main impediment to his doing this is not, as you might think, getting the fish to write the poetry, but in getting anyone else to take their work seriously.

For many years now, Rollie Zerbs has been going to the end of the pier below his blufftop house every day and checking the paper in his old Royal typewriter, which he leaves out whenever weather and river allow. What he's done is attach lines of differing length to each key on that typewriter and let them down into the water, hooked and baited. Periodically a fish will yank on one of those lines and depress a key on the typewriter. And gradually, over the course of weeks and months and years, the fish have wound up writing things.

Just about everybody in LaPorte has walked at one time or another out onto the pier and looked at what the fish were up to, and just about everybody has pointed out to Uncle Rollie that the stuff on the pages isn't any good. I've been out there several times and the only actual word I ever saw spelled out correctly was "wart." Most of it looks like the kind of thing your baby daughter does when she gets at the keys. I've seen no indication of any talent of any kind on the part of any of these fish.

It's not much use bringing that up to Uncle Rollie, however. It doesn't have any effect on him. He sits on his porch, on the small bluff overlooking the river, and pays more attention to the mosquitoes than he does to criticism. He's squatty and squish-faced, with thick spiky black hair and glasses and a stumpy cigar. He's ugly, but he's not alarming at all—he doesn't look crazy or dangerous. In fact if anything he looks kind of satisfied. Superior. And if, as I say, you mention your doubts as to the ability of his fish, he just points with his cigar out to the end of the pier and tells you this:

"You got to be patient with 'em is all. What in

the hell do you expect, accurate spelling? Jeee-sus Ka-RIST. They're underwater! The best they can do is *guess* which line goes to which key. That's where I come in. If after a few days I see what appears to be just drunken nonsense, something like 'fjeighexlskeh,' well, I look all through that to see if there's a word anywhere. Now, you see, there's one. 'Hex.' Well, all right then. I keep that word and throw out all the errors. And you keep all the words and put them together and you'll end up sometimes at the end of a few months with something so fine and mysterious that it haunts your dreams. You can't tell *me* those fish don't know what they're doin'. They're *deep*."

And then he'll haul out some of the poems. I remember one in particular he showed me. He'd "cleaned up all the mistakes," and it read like this:

> *He ran not out from*
> *But into under*
> *The falling shards*

Uncle Rollie has enough of these to make up a small volume, and he's perpetually sending copies of it to publishers with a standing invitation for them to come out to LaPorte and see for themselves that he's telling the truth and the material is actually being written by freshwater fish, mostly perch. So far nobody's taken him up on it, but I know that he's on the square because I've been on the pier late at night when a couple of those keys have hammered on the page, and I'll testify it's an eerie experience.

3

Uncle Rollie's gotten to the point where he doesn't really expect his fish poetry to be recognized or acknowledged in his lifetime. "Most people," he says, "don't know gold when it's in the street; they only know it when it's in the store window." He's accustomed to being looked upon as a figure of fun. Once a year they send somebody over from the Quincy, Illinois, TV news, across the river, and do a feature about him, "On the Lighter Side." But he sees himself as basically a serious person with a calling, not like these people who swallow their noses on videotape to get on TV.

The consensus in LaPorte has always been that Rollie Zerbs is claiming for the fish of the Mississippi a talent they don't possess, and that he shouldn't make them work at a job they're not qualified for.

But no one's ever tried to stop him. He's always been allowed to pursue happiness in his own way—until now.

Now, it seems, Uncle Rollie is in danger of being closed down. He just called to tell me about it. He's looking my way for assistance—one Zerbs to another. He thinks we're a lot alike.

He wants me to come back to LaPorte and help him out. He says my mother is trying to put him away, and that I'm the only one he can count on.

He called me up tonight and said, "Cooper, your mother says I've got diminished capacity."

"I don't see how that's possible, Uncle Rollie," I said.

This whole question of Rollie Zerbs's mind has been a reliable subject of conversation in LaPorte for years, like the weather or the Cardinals. But the idea of him deteriorating from his usual level has never come up.

"Your mother is comin' at me from every angle here," he told me.

My mom has never completely forgiven herself for marrying into the LaPorte Zerbses. My dad Loren, Uncle Rollie's little brother, was a failure by most standards, including his own. He left us when I was a kid, but he was so unsuccessful in his travels that he came back. Mom had to ask him to go away again. There has never been a Zerbs in LaPorte who excited much admiration.

Mom, on the other hand, is a Tyke, and the Tykes tend to do well and accomplish things. One of my cousins, Charlie Tyke, played shortstop for Chicago in the major leagues for several years. He's the most famous person to come out of LaPorte. Mom herself has artistic talent. She wrote and illustrated a history of northeast Missouri for the DAR.

People in town think the Tykes and Zerbses should never have merged. They've always viewed me as a kind of checkerboard on which the influences of the two families are canceling themselves out.

When I was growing up, it was suggested from time to time by other kids in town that I should be ashamed of myself for being a Zerbs. But Mom always encouraged me, and I tried extra hard to amount to something and get out of LaPorte. Eventually I ended up here in Chicago, where I've found a little niche for myself at the Neatly Chiseled Features newspaper syndicate.

But even when I was embarrassed about him and denying that we were blood relatives, I always liked my uncle. I won't say he was a role model. I never wanted to emulate Uncle Rollie. I got my role models from the TV and the sports pages. But I liked him anyway. He liked me, too. When I was little, he sat me up on the bar in his tavern and gave me pretzels. Later on he took me down to Busch Stadium twice a year to see the Cardinals.

I always wished, though, that he'd drop the fish thing.

It didn't surprise me to hear tonight that my mom is trying to get Uncle Rollie under supervision. She considers herself responsible for family, even old cracked ex-in-laws. During the big flood a couple years ago, when Uncle Rollie had to move to higher ground, he stayed in her backyard cottage on the upper bluff. It was then that her opinion of him solidified.

Nor was I surprised that Uncle Rollie called me up about it.

"I knew you'd understand how it feels," he said.

I've got a little of that myself, is what he meant. A little diminished capacity. I used to be noteworthy in the family for my quick, retentive mind, but I hit my head on a building in an incident here in Chicago last winter and ever since then I haven't been at full strength mentally. I have gaps. Sometimes my head feels dense inside. It isn't painful but it's distracting.

At work, at Neatly Chiseled Features, I don't do as much as I used to. I mostly just read the comics now. I check to make sure the words in the balloons are spelled right and the arrows are pointing at the right characters. I log the features in and out. We have about forty different comic strips and panels, which we sell to newspapers all over the country. I also go through the submissions to see if any show promise. We get about a thousand submissions a year from cartoonists who want to be syndicated.

It's a position of some responsibility, but I don't kid myself. They don't consider me sharp enough anymore to proofread the daily text features. You can sit there and take your time with two weeks of The Careful Avenger or Wacky Kat, but you have to turn the political columns around in an hour. I just can't do that anymore. If there's any kind of deadline or intellectual pressure, I get that feeling of density in my head. Sometimes I can't retain the sense of what I'm reading from paragraph to paragraph. My doctor says I'm making progress, but it's been slow.

I saw a TV newsmagazine story once about a man who ate some bad shellfish and lost his short-term memory. He had to write down everything he did all day or he'd forget where he was going and where he was coming from. My impairment isn't nearly that extensive, but since I saw that story I've taken to keeping a record of things, as a safety measure. I try to write things down while they're fresh. My recollection isn't photographic, like it used to be.

Now it's more smeared, like an Impressionist painting. But by writing events down as I go along, if I get worse at least I'll be able to read my own memoirs and find out what I did.

I've retained most of what Uncle Rollie said tonight. His main concern is that Mom wants to have him put in a home.

"She's discovered a place out near Medina that costs thirty-eight dollars a day and doesn't take overflow from the mental hospital," he said. "How's that sound? Pretty good?"

"She told you that?" I asked him.

"Says I'm going to burn my house down. I guess I can burn down the goddamn house if I want to."

"Do you want to?"

"What are you doin', Cooper, testing to find out if I'm an idiot?"

Uncle Rollie doesn't want to leave his house because his "work" is there, down below on the pier. He evacuated during the flood when the water covered the kitchen floor, but he came back afterward, through the silt and the gumbo. He is impervious to advice and ridicule.

"People don't think that fish poetry of yours is very rational," I told him at one point tonight.

"Well, I'll tell ya," he said. "Your mother and her friends think in the year 2000 Jesus is gonna come down out of the sky on a horse."

"That's religion," I said.

"Well, who's to say Jesus ain't coachin' my fish?" he demanded. "Maybe they're harbingers of the Judg-

8

ment Day. Maybe they're gonna give us the Word from out of the rolling river."

"I suppose you talk like that around Mom."

There was a pause. When Uncle Rollie spoke again he was quieter and a little shaky.

"I wish you'd come on down here, Cooper," he said. "I got people comin' in here when I'm asleep."

I couldn't make anything of that.

"Who?" I asked.

"Cooper," he said, "it would be*hoove* you to do me this favor."

I got that. That meant I owe him, because I let him down previously by not submitting his fish poetry to my boss. Uncle Rollie thinks a daily fish poem would be an attractive feature in the nation's newspapers. But I've never felt secure enough in my job to present the idea to my superiors.

So he said again, "It would be*hoove* you. I can maybe ride this out if you'll just . . . come down here and do this one thing for me that I've got in mind." And then he added gruffly, "Please," and hung up on me.

Mom called up about a half hour later and told me Uncle Rollie has senile dementia.

"Your uncle has accelerated deterioration of the remainder of his mind," she said. "I'm going to need you to come down here and help me, we're going to have to get a conservatorship. There's nobody on your father's side of the family left in town, so we have to do it. There might have to be a hearing."

"Well, I just talked to him and he didn't sound so bad," I said.

"He's got enough adrenaline left to sound borderline, briefly," she said, "but that's all. What did he want? What did he say to you?"

"He wanted me to come down and visit," I said.

"Good," she said. "He likes you and he might listen to you. Come on and be a help. It's time you participated in the family."

I've got a week's vacation coming. I worry about being out of the office because I'm afraid my substitute will outshine me, but Casey has always said my job is secure, and he has no reason to lie to me. He could have fired me when I started making mistakes after I hit my head, but he didn't.

Here at home . . . well, I don't think the idea of a trip to Missouri will be popular. Irene's been there once before. She didn't like it.

We're still living together, but Irene's not real pleased with me. Seems like she's mad all the time. I don't like to live like that. I can't get my balance when I'm in the sitting room, wondering whether she's going to come in at me from the kitchen or the bedroom. She circles around the apartment and then darts in and grabs something of mine off an end table and takes it away and puts it somewhere else.

Off balance; that's it. That's the way I feel at home. About once a winter I take a big fall on the ice, usually when I'm coming up the walk with two bags of groceries. One heel slips and I try to recover with the other one and then *it* slips and I get to backpedaling and my arms go shooting up and the groceries sail up in the air as I land on my tailbone on the pavement. It's a satisfying sight to the passerby. Sometimes if I have time before I land I say, "Woo-woo-woo!"

That's how it is with Irene. Inside I'm always saying, "Woo-woo-woo."

She's asleep now. I guess I'll wait to tell her about this. She said something recently about us going to Lake Geneva on my vacation. LaPorte isn't really comparable.

Uncle Rollie seemed about the same except for that part about people sneaking up on him while he's asleep. That didn't sound like he was razor-sharp.

It never occurred to me that somebody like him could slow down. People talk about how sad it is to see the ruin of a noble mind, but it's sad, to me, to think of the ruin of Uncle Rollie's mind, too.

CHAPTER TWO

It's late Tuesday night, the TV has signed off and I'm in Uncle Rollie's sitting room in LaPorte. I'm still a little rattled. My arrival was more eventful than I wanted it to be.

I didn't have any problem yesterday, getting permission to come down here. At work, Casey just said, "Take all the time you need." He didn't even ask me why I had to go.

He may have been preoccupied, thinking about the Cubs. They're even with the Dodgers in the National League playoffs, two wins apiece. Casey lives a major portion of his life through them. He keeps an old Billy Williams bat in his office, and when his schedule allows, he watches the Cubs on a small black-and-white TV, standing with the bat and adjusting his stance to mimic each Chicago hitter. He swings when they swing and takes when they take.

That's what he was doing when I went in to see

him. He wished me luck and told me not to worry about anything. Then he grounded into a double play, and I went home to face Irene.

She's still mad. There's a problem between us that we can't get over. Irene's disappointed in me because I'm not as dynamic as I originally seemed. I misled her at the beginning of our relationship by doing something heroic.

It was one of those unlikely, pivotal incidents. I think everybody has a few. The kind you look back on and say, "Well, if I hadn't gone out drinking the night they tore down the Berlin Wall, I wouldn't have met Vonetta and Russell Jr. would never have been born."

What happened was this: About seven months ago when we were still just acquaintances, I raced out into the night to try and protect her from her big angry drunken estranged boyfriend Stan. And although I didn't afford much protection—in fact I got my head trauma—Irene got it into *her* head that I was exciting and fiery. While the truth is I like it quiet. Especially since that incident.

Now we've been together for a few months, and she's seen me watching RKO Classic Movie Theater on TV. She knows the truth.

It's fashionable these days to look down on people who stay at home, to say they should get a life. But if we were all running around outside there'd be nothing but collisions. I believe some of us were meant to be noisy and kinetic, and others of us were meant to be more contemplative and inert.

Of course, I'd like a woman beside me with similar views. When I lived in LaPorte I had a girlfriend named Charlotte Prine who would be just right for me as I am now. But back then, I wanted so badly to get out of town and succeed at something that I didn't pay enough attention to her. Next thing I knew she'd gone and married Lloyd Wiemeier and it just ate me alive. I still see her in my dreams.

Irene likes to go out. I can see why she's frustrated with me. If I'd been in my right mind when we first got together I would have warned her, but I was suffering from the effects of that blow to the head and I apparently acted more interesting than I am.

The fun's pretty much over now, though. She's impatient with my memory lapses, and our sex life is suffering. I'm usually too embarrassed to talk about sex except during it, but in this case I should mention it to complete the picture. We're just not clawing our way to ecstasy like she tells me we used to.

It turned out to be simple to work out the vacation situation tonight. She didn't even mention Lake Geneva. I told her I was thinking of going to Missouri and she said, "Fine. You should go. In fact, you should stay."

She went on a little more; I can't recall it all, so I've condensed her response. She finished by saying, "If you don't wake up pretty soon you can forget about me."

The truth is that the way my head feels lately, I probably *can* forget about her.

* * *

One of the disadvantages to LaPorte in my youth was that you could only get two stations on TV. ABC didn't have an affiliate. There was CBS and NBC and sitting on the porch. They've still only got two stations locally. The more well-to-do people have cable, but Uncle Rollie is not one of those people.

There are compensations. The air is fresh here. There's a spacious feeling; everybody's got a yard. I like that now. I've been in Chicago long enough to lose my fascination with great clusters of people.

It's comforting to think that with all the overpopulation and crowding everywhere, with people jamming themselves into suburbs and even into places like Montana and Wyoming, that nobody is trying to get into LaPorte. It's safe from being exploited because there's no economy.

The Farm Barn outlet moved to Quincy and the Fairfax Gypsum plant closed down. There's farmland and a little ballpark on the edge of town, a school, a couple gas stations, three taverns, the bank, a 7-Eleven, and a market. That's about it.

River people used to dock at the pier in front of Thorpe's Boathouse to gas up and get a beer and a burger, but after Thorpe passed away the boathouse got flooded out and just fell apart. There's no place to dock in LaPorte these days.

The population was 1100 when I was a boy and it's 937 now.

I got into town around 7:30, and stopped at the 7-Eleven on Front Street to pick up some soda pop in case Mom didn't have any up at the house. And of course the first person I saw was Charlotte. She was shopping with her son.

It hit me a solid blow, seeing her. Some girls from high school, you see them years later and kind of thank your stars you missed out. But Charlotte's still fit. Her face is a bit fuller but that doesn't hurt her any in my estimation. I don't care so much for the angular faces with the skin stretched over the bone like a drumhead, anymore.

Her boy Dillon is nine years old now. He's named after the old James Arness character on "Gunsmoke."

She acted pleased to see me. She told Dillon my name and he shook hands with me.

"You carried my mom home when she broke her leg at Dyer's farm," Dillon told me solemnly.

"Well . . ." I said.

It's true. I was six and Charlotte was four. She broke it on the swingset in the Dyers' backyard.

"Dillon knows all the family history," Charlotte said.

"And the bone didn't set right and that's why you walk like you do," he added tactlessly to his mother. Charlotte has a slightly exaggerated amble when she walks.

"No," she said, giving him a shove. "Not anymore, anyway. Somebody said it was sexy and now I do it on purpose."

Dillon went off to look at the cereals, and Charlotte said, "I hear you edit 'Tell It to Jeanne.'"

"Who told you that?"

"Your mom."

"Well . . . I don't anymore. I mostly read comic strips now."

"Still, there you are, up in Chicago like you wanted."

"What's Lloyd up to?" I asked.

"Who cares?" she said, and laughed.

Charlotte's an oil painter now. She's done portraits of people in Quincy, across the river. She's got an appointment in Chicago in a couple days to submit one of her landscapes to a new restaurant chain that's going to feature genetically toughened vegetables. If they like her painting they're going to hang a print in every franchise.

She asked if I'd brought Irene down with me and I said no. Before we split up she asked, "Do you really know Roger Ebert?"

"I've met him," I said modestly.

"Can't beat that," she said, and rolled on with her cart.

I got a pleasant, melancholy feeling, driving up the big hill to Mom's house.

She lives in the Tyke family home, on the Upper Bluff overlooking town and the river, in a yard full of walnut trees. Grampa Tyke made sure the house was maintained while he was alive so Mom would have a place to stay no matter what Dad failed at.

At one time or another Dad was a salesman, a trucker, and a manager of a hardware store in West Quincy, but he always struck me as a frustrated performer. He probably should have gone into show business. His passion was comedy.

I remember once when I was a boy, he drove Mom and me down to Hannibal to Mark Twain's Cave. That's the big tourist attraction in Northeast Missouri, you know. It's a labyrinth stuck in the hills south of town. In *Tom Sawyer*, Tom and Becky Thatcher got lost in it and Injun Joe died in it. It's got a nice little gift shop attached to it now, with guided tours through the main passage all day.

The guides always do pretty much the same thing, follow the same route and give the same speech, about Tom and Becky and the bats. About halfway through, when you're deep inside the cave, they turn out all the lights for ten seconds or so, so you can see how dark it is. And it *is* dark; it's black.

The time we went, Dad, Mom, and I were in the rear of the group when the lights went out. And when they came back on, Dad had disappeared. It's fairly easy to do; there are all kinds of tributaries off the main tunnel. You just take a few steps down one and you're gone.

I'm not sure what he expected Mom to do. Raise the alarm, I suppose. And then he'd reappear and tell some story about a clutching hand or falling in a hole or something.

But Mom didn't raise the alarm. She looked around, took a deep breath through her nose, and hauled me on with the rest of the group. We came out in the gift shop. I was very worried about Dad, I remember. Mom bought me a wooden gun that shot rubber bands and then drove us home in the Olds-mobile.

Dad stayed in the cave for a while, living a kind of a comedian's nightmare, I imagine: you make your joke and then stand alone in pitch-black silence. He eventually merged into the back of the next tour group, making one kid scream, and went on through. He had to hitch back to LaPorte. He was mad when he got home.

I can see both sides. Mom was justified in reject-ing Dad's humor as too heavy, but it was tough on him, too; it's hard when your best stuff isn't going over. I've seen how these cartoonists suffer watching me read their comic submissions. Like Mom, I rarely laugh. I think it's because we've both seen so *many* jokes.

Dad left home not long after that. Mom has al-ways said she was relieved. I don't think there is any subconscious contradiction beneath the statement. She and I moved in with Grampa Tyke. Dad came back now and then for brief visits before he passed away in 1979 from liver death. Mom inherited money from Grampa when *he* died in '89, so she's secure.

She wasn't home when I got up the hill, so I sat on the porch while the lightning bugs came out. I'd just heard an item on the radio about them. You know times are hard locally when they do a story about a company down in St. Louis buying lightning bugs at a penny apiece for some research purpose, and then they repeat the story because the station switchboard's been flooded with calls asking where to send them.

I thought maybe Mom had told me to meet her someplace and I'd forgotten. I decided to drive down the hill and up the road to Uncle Rollie's place.

He lives on the Lower Bluff, in a clapboard house beside a crushed gravel road that runs parallel to the river. He's on the left, up at the end of the road, after you go by the big grain silo, in a small cleared patch under the trees.

His lights were on and Mom's car was parked in the yard when I drove up. I parked behind her and got out.

There's only one other dwelling there, just this side of Uncle Rollie's. It's a mobile home. Wendell Kendall lives in it.

Parking as I did, behind Mom's car, I was between the two buildings, so it wasn't clear who I was visiting. And I neglected to call out to Wendell to let him know it was me.

Wendell is about Uncle Rollie's age—upper seventies. He's a short, skinny old man of the type you seem to find mostly in the country, with sunken cheeks and thick glasses and an old Cardinal cap on every minute of the day. He's walked slowly since I was a boy. Now he's getting frail. He's still dangerous, though.

Wendell's the nicest guy in the state if he sees you coming. He'll talk your head sore about his workshop and where he purchased his circular saw. There's not the least bit of harm in him if he knows you.

But he's been living alone for years, with no near neighbors except Uncle Rollie and the grain silo. That and guilt have been eating away at his reason.

When he was young, Wendell worked briefly at the Fairfax Gypsum plant on the other side of town. As I understand it, he stole a tool from them. Embezzled it, you might say. I don't know what it was. Maybe a hammer. He may have done it in retaliation for getting laid off, or he may have just been unable to resist it. Wendell loves tools.

Anyway, nothing happened; nobody caught him. He eventually went to work somewhere else.

Not much of a story, except that over the course of the ensuing fifty-five years, Wendell has allowed it to grow and overcome him. He believes now that he's on a list for retaliation. He believes that one of these nights some old-time strikebreaker types from the plant are going to drive down to the end of the gravel road and call him out. His crime has earned interest in his head. It's become one of those for which there is no statute of limitations. It doesn't matter to Wendell that the Fairfax Gypsum plant has been closed now for years. As far as he's concerned that's just a stratagem.

Uncle Rollie is tolerant of Wendell's obsession, living, as you might say, next door, in a glass house. But it has made him uneasy in recent years because it seems to have gotten more intense and because Wendell has always said he'll shoot it out with them when they come. Wendell is well armed, like many Missourians. You go out to a swap meet in the countryside and you'll find enough rifles on sale to repel any neighboring state.

Uncle Rollie doesn't approve of fixed ideas that make a person sit up at night by the window with a shotgun in his lap. I've heard him yell across his yard, "One of these days they're gonna come, Wendell, only they ain't gonna be from the Fairfax plant."

Well, sure enough, I got about four steps away from the car and there was a flash and a "BOOM" and a crash and I swear, I thought I'd disintegrated. I thought I'd somehow blown up, it was that loud and unexpected. On the way to the ground I thought of lightning; we get some frightening storms in La-Porte in the summer. But no, the night was clear; it was Wendell shooting my car.

It's a brown Dodge Colt Premier. I bought it used. He'd never seen it before. As my senses returned to me I realized that I had been at fault, and from my position facedown in the grass I screamed, "It's *Coo*-per!"

Uncle Rollie's door opened ahead of me and the light from the kitchen shone into the yard. I raised my head and started to crawl toward the door. Mom came out. Uncle Rollie stood in the doorway in his pj's.

Mom did the initial talking. She is a Tyke and prefers to act dignified, but she can make herself heard over the crickets all right. She's gotten kind of stocky as she's gotten older. You can't miss her.

"Cooper!" she barked, walking up to me. "Have you lost your *mind*? Can't you sing *out*?"

Off to my left, Wendell, looking skinnier and flimsier than ever, opened his trailer door. He had trouble getting down the steps and out his door with the shotgun. He got the bill of his cap turned in the door frame and involuntarily pointed the gun at Mom.

"Don't you point that thing at me," she said. She strode up to him and began wrestling him for it. "I'll turn it on you, Wendell, I swear. You let . . . *go*."

He did, and she stood there, panting at him, holding the shotgun backward and down at her right side.

"I didn't know the car," Wendell said finally.

"So you shot it," said Mom.

"Who is it? Cooper?" said Uncle Rollie, out in the yard now. He walked up to me in his pj's. They were big on him; he's lost the big belly he used to have. He looked happy to see me, but confused and old without his glasses. His hair was sticking out at the sides like he'd had an electric shock.

I stood up and shook hands with him.

"Nobody is coming for you," Mom was saying emphatically to Wendell, jabbing the butt of his shotgun at him. "Nobody knows you're alive except us."

Uncle Rollie said, "What'd he do, shoot at Cooper?"

"*Yes*, he shot at Cooper," said Mom. "He thinks everybody who drives down this road is from the Fairfax Gypsum plant."

Uncle Rollie peered toward Wendell and said, "Goddamn it, Wendell, you're goin' nuts."

Wendell said, "I was only doin' what you told me."

Uncle Rollie blinked and snapped his head back as though he'd received a short jab. This is his customary reaction to astounding news.

Then he looked at me and said, "What are *you* doin' here?"

Wendell's back in his trailer, Mom's gone home up the hill, and Uncle Rollie's in bed. He's tired out.

After we went in the house he and Mom got into an argument about whether he'd forgotten I was coming. Uncle Rollie denied it, but Mom outlasted him and spent some time describing his symptoms to me while he sat with us in the kitchen.

"He leaves the oven on," she said. "He puts a piece of meat in there and walks away and forgets about it. Look at the oven door. *Look* at it."

"I see it."

"I don't understand why he's still alive. The meat's rotten to begin with. I came over here with Maisie Dupree to clean out his refrigerator and we were here two days. The man is a derelict."

"BULLshit!" barked Uncle Rollie. Mom sailed on.

"We took a cheese out of there that was given to him Christmas before last. He's watching us. He says, 'I for*got* about *that*,' and takes a *fork* to it. In front of Maisie. I thought I'd die. I thought *he'd* die. I don't know why the three of us didn't just expire on the spot."

Uncle Rollie sat on a kitchen chair and stared at

the table. He seemed dazed.

"He's not drinking," said Mom, "but then, the way he is now, he doesn't have to."

Uncle Rollie used to drink, to an extent that's considered excessive nowadays. I remember him telling me once about the merits of "sippin' gin." He also loved Stag and Falstaff, two beers you don't hear much about anymore.

"He sleeps eighteen hours a day. All he does— here's what he does. He gets up, he goes down to that rickety old pier and looks at that—*crap* in the typewriter, and then he drives into Quincy to see Callie."

"He drives over there every day?"

"In low. He leaves the car in low the whole way. I'm surprised the *car* is still alive. His license has expired, his insurance is canceled, and he has *no* chance of passing the driver's test. He won't pay his bills anymore. He says they don't add up right and he'll figure them out tomorrow."

"They *don't* add up right," said Uncle Rollie.

"How come he's got lights?"

"He's got lights because *I* went over and paid Nancy Asher personally at the GE collections office. And don't think she's not telling the world."

Mom got up, looking a little tired herself. I always think of her as young; her hair is still the same auburn it always was. But her face is getting lined and leathery.

"I'm going home," she said. "You should stay here, Cooper."

"I intended to," I said, and looked at Uncle Rollie. "Okay with you?" I asked. He looked up at me and smiled vaguely.

"Good," said Mom. "You can see what I'm talking about." She bent over toward him and said distinctly, "I'm leaving, Roland."

"I'll get over it," he said.

CHAPTER THREE

Along about 3 a.m. I was settled on the couch in the sitting room, under an old army blanket, when Uncle Rollie began to stir upstairs, bumping around.

Ordinarily I wouldn't have heard him; I sleep well as a rule. But Wendell had shaken me up so I was still half ready to jump.

I got up off the couch and walked to the stairs and called up, "Uncle Rollie?"

"Cooper? You awake?"

"Well, yeah."

"C'mon up here."

I went up the old stairs. They always remind me what a poor housekeeper Uncle Rollie is. Halfway up the steps the ceiling goes vertical, up to the second story ceiling, and I always take a look above me at that point because once when I was a boy I came upstairs and there on the plaster over my head was a big black snake—three or four feet long—stuck on the wall, asleep. I didn't see it until I got to the top and turned around. It must have liked the cool surface in the heat.

I'm not generally critical about how other people keep house, but I remember hollering about that. Uncle Rollie came out of his room and apologized for not noticing the snake earlier. He knocked it off the wall with a shovel; it went into the closet under the stairs. Uncle Rollie said reptiles were one of the drawbacks of living near the river.

Tonight there was no snake, but the state of Uncle Rollie's room was almost as big a shock. Mom had said it was a mess, but I wasn't prepared for the extent of it.

The first thing you noticed on entering the room was that for months Uncle Rollie had been buying the Chicago and St. Louis papers and reading them in bed. Then he had put them down. Now he had to put them *up*. There were stacks all over the room, leaning against each other. You couldn't reach the bed except by a narrow diagonal path from the door.

Uncle Rollie was sitting up on his favorite side of the mattress. I could tell it was his favorite side because it had a crater in it to accommodate his rump.

"I've read about people like you," I said. "Found in their rooms under a pile of cat food cans. They usually turn out to be worth ten or eleven million dollars."

He was writing on a legal pad with one Bic pen and sucking on another. He had a thermos of something on the bedside table next to him.

"Listen to this," he said, and cleared his throat for about fifteen seconds.

"Pretty good," I said.

"Shut up." He pushed his glasses up on his nose and read from the legal pad, "Time is the guest of the north."

He set the pad down on his lap and looked at me. "Whaddya think of that?"

"I don't understand it."

"I don't either," said Uncle Rollie, frowning down at the pad. "I think I misinterpreted it. It's close, though. These fish are on the verge of a breakthrough."

I bent down and pushed over a pile of newspapers to see the date on the bottom one.

"What are you doin'?" said Uncle Rollie.

"Want to see if the Browns are still in St. Louis."

"You sound like your mother. If I want to keep my room a mess I can do it."

"You've proved that."

Uncle Rollie laboriously swung his legs over the side and creaked out of bed.

"C'mon," he said.

He led me slowly back down the stairs and into a moldy old room on the river side of the house that's always been used to collect mildew and old furniture. Uncle Rollie lives in his bedroom, the kitchen, and the sitting room.

The room was dark. Uncle Rollie flicked on the wall switch and nothing happened.

"You can't see it, but that window over near the

corner's busted in," he said. "The lock's busted on one of the windows over there."

"Somebody broke in?" I asked.

"Somebody's broke in every night for a week. I finally told Wendell if he's gonna wait for the goblins from Fairfax Gypsum, he should sit up for these goddamned thieves, too."

He left the room and went down the hall to the kitchen, where he picked up a flashlight, opened the door, and walked outside. I followed him to the doorway and stopped, reluctant to go out in the yard.

Uncle Rollie looked back at me and said, "Oh." Then he hollered, "GOIN' TO THE PIER WITH COOPER!"

I accompanied Uncle Rollie down the slope in front of the house. The moon was full and shining a path across the river toward us. Once on the pier I followed his steps exactly in case of rotten slats, and we walked out to the end, where his Royal typewriter sits atop a rectangular hole just beyond a folding aluminum picnic chair.

Uncle Rollie sat down in the chair, leaned over, and trained his flash on the paper in the typewriter.

"Nothin'." He sighed and sat back. "Stubborn."

"Who's breaking into the house?" I asked him.

"I don't know, but I know *why*." He looked up at me. "Your mother probably gave you several verses tonight about my habits." He didn't seem to remember having sat there while she did it.

"She's worried about you."

"I hope to hell you'll excuse me, Cooper, but

your mother is a goddamned meddler, and I could put it stronger. She pecks and pokes and pries at people until they'd rather be on fire. It's because she didn't go into a public career. She shoulda run for the assembly or invented some new kind of surgical instrument."

"I don't go for remarks about my mother," I said. I was a little stiff about it.

"Well, I didn't mean to go on," said Uncle Rollie. "The point I'm tryin' to make . . . the reason I brought it up . . . oh, hell." He looked out over the water again. "There was a reason I brought it up and now I can't think of it."

I couldn't either, so I sat down cross-legged on the pier and we were quiet for a little while. Everything was quiet for a little while. Then one of the keys struck the typewriter ribbon and I jumped. We both leaned forward and saw that it was an "F."

Uncle Rollie grunted. "Good," he said. "Don't have much use for x's and z's." He joggled the line and it went slack again.

"What makes you think these fish write in English?" I asked him.

"Well, they ain't heard any French around here in two hundred years," he said. He waved out at the river. "If these fish have been granted a gift, why, then they'll communicate in the language we can best understand, ain't that logical? Ain't they God's creatures? Ain't this God's river? Listen up, Cooper, prepare yourself. Come a day you're gonna be surprised and enlightened."

We sat there a minute or so longer and then Uncle Rollie heard something. I didn't. He twisted in his seat and growled at me.

"Get up quiet."

I did so. I couldn't hear anything but crickets.

"Go along the river and see if there's anybody outside the house."

I walked back until I reached the bank, then stepped off the pier and trotted parallel to the water until I tripped and fell. After that I walked.

I heard Uncle Rollie back around the corner of the house to my right, yelling at Wendell, "Goddamn it, you shoot at my nephew and you sleep through the robbers!"

Wendell's lights came on behind me, and as they did somebody came out of Uncle Rollie's front door, up the slope from the riverbank. I was shocked. I was so used to thinking of Uncle Rollie as deluded that I couldn't accept it right away.

I was scandalized, really. I thought it showed some nerve, breaking into the house of a poor, harmless, demented old man. I couldn't understand it. It was bad sportsmanship; it was bad judgment. There wasn't any future in it. What was he after? The old newspapers? The cheese? Was he just practicing?

He needed the practice, I thought. He was noisy, he was heavy on his feet, and he was wearing a white T-shirt. I couldn't tell if I knew him or not. Uncle Rollie said later that he's so casual because he's overfamiliar with breaking into the house. He about punches in and out.

On this occasion he actually slammed the door behind him and stomped off the porch and around the corner toward the woods at the end of the road. He *was* careful to keep the house between himself and Wendell's trailer.

I scrambled up the slope after him, hollering "Hey!" like a fool. He broke into a run at the edge of the woods and was gone by the time I got there.

"They're tryin' to get my card."

Uncle Rollie and I were back in the kitchen, sitting on these high wicker-seat chairs he used to have in his tavern instead of bar stools. He was snacking on some old stale popcorn.

"I did a damn fool thing," he told me. "I shoulda called you first. But I took it to Quincy, to a card store. I showed it to this kid and asked him what it was worth. He said he didn't know 'cause it wasn't in the price guide." Uncle Rollie chewed on his popcorn. "He told somebody."

"You've got a baseball card?" I asked him.

Uncle Rollie's head snapped back with the shock.

"Catch up, Cooper," he said. "How many times do I have to tell ya?"

"At least once," I said.

"I ain't told ya about the card?"

"I'm not sure. I don't think so."

"*Damn.* C'mere then."

He started me on a little tour of the hiding places in the house. "I got to see where I put it," he said. "I had it here"—he showed me an old cookie tin in the sitting room—"but then when they broke in the first time I moved it."

I was thinking we should invite the robber over to help us out; we were all in the same wilderness. Wandering through the house, looking in the chest of drawers, rummaging through boxes, taking books out of the bookcases and flipping through the pages. Uncle Rollie has acquired all sorts of knickknacks and junk.

"I had a fella come in and appraise this stuff and he told me it was all worthless," he said. We started upstairs to look in the bedroom.

"My daddy, your grampa Zerbs, lived in Chicago when he was younger, and he liked the Cubs," he went on. "They had a great team back then. This is the Frank Chance Cubs I'm talkin' about.

"Back then Detroit had Cobb, and Pittsburgh had Wagner. And the Cubs had Tinker and Evers and Chance." Uncle Rollie pronounced it "EE-vers."

"In nineteen-seven the Cubs beat Cobb and the Tigers in the World Series. And the next year they beat Cobb and the Tigers in the World Series again. So they were world champions for two years in a row. And they never been since."

He was in his room now, huffing and puffing through the newspapers around his bed, trying to work his way over to his big desk in the corner.

"My daddy liked cigars," he said. "Roberto Higueras. Robertos, they called 'em. And in nineteen-nine the Robertos people put pictures of nine Cubs in their cigar boxes because they were world champions.

Every box had one Cub inside. They had Tinker and Evers and Chance and Steinfeldt, Sheckard and Hofman and Kling, and Three Finger Brown. And they had Daddy's favorite player—" Uncle Rollie gave a big grunt, seeing something ahead of him, and bulled his way through to his desk.

I followed through the path he'd made and looked over his shoulder down at the desktop. There was a lot of dust and dirt and paperwork—Uncle Rollie's recent phone, electric, and car insurance bills; his tax return, unsigned, unsent, and six months late; old keys with pieces of yarn attached to them; a doorknob; some yellow sheets with fish writing on them; old photographs of Zerbses in tiny oval frames; cork coasters; rubber bands and change and old stamps. And an old book with a floral pattern on the cover, bound with a ropy kind of string. Uncle Rollie opened it up and flipped past some pages covered with handwriting and got to the middle, where he uncovered a stiff piece of board. He flipped it over.

Underneath, in a soft plastic sleeve, was a little, shiny, pastel-colored picture of a young fellow with a tiny cap, a big strong nose, and a genial kind of squint.

"Wildfire Schulte," said Uncle Rollie.

I could hear the crickets outside again. I stared at the picture. It looked like a big stamp. It said "F. Schulte, Chi." on the bottom.

"Did I read about this?"

"They ain't supposed to be any of these left," said Uncle Rollie. "Not in this good of a condition.

They've got good ones of all the others, but not Schulte. It was in the Chicago papers. Now, you live up there in Illinois." He pronounced the "s" at the end. "You know how the old Cub fans are. It's like they've got a disease."

"I know."

"And on top of that they've got these collectors. If you took it up there, one of 'em might pay a few thousand for it. And with that money, you see, I could get somebody to come in here and clean house so your mother might let me alone."

He shut the album on "F. Schulte, Chi." and blinked at the wall.

"I'm a little scared of her," he said quietly. "Way she talks about 'benign confinement.' "

He sat down on his bed and peered up at me.

"Whose side are you on here, Cooper?"

CHAPTER FOUR

I called Casey at work in Chicago and he said he'd get back to me on the Roberto Higuera card set of 1909.

That's a pretty good card, I'll bet. It's remarkable that Uncle Rollie would turn out to have it.

For years everybody in LaPorte has looked upon him as a half-length in front of Wendell Kendall in the race for town crackpot. One time the boys down at the basement tavern decided Uncle Rollie was the strangest man in the entire state, but he wouldn't accept the honor; he said it was just a popularity contest. Now the whole town's broke and Uncle Rollie's sitting on a shrewd investment. You just never know who's going to turn out to be smart.

Or what's going to turn out to be valuable. If Mom hadn't thrown out my old cards years ago in the name of clutter removal, I'd have a valuable collection myself. I kept them in a green tackle box. I knew them so well you could lift one up just a little bit, just reveal a sliver below the top border, and I could tell you who it was. He didn't have to be a star. Just show me a strip of sky, and I'd say, "Galen Cisco" or "Gene Brabender" and I'd be right.

Made me kind of ill when they went shooting up in value like that in the '80s. I kept track of the prices for a while but then I couldn't stand it anymore.

But if I can get good money for this card, Uncle Rollie can hire a keeper. He can go to the river and look at that typewriter until his intellect just trickles away entirely, and no harm done.

Yesterday morning we went to the DMV in Ewing in Uncle Rollie's old pickup so he could take the driver's test. He didn't make it to the driving part. He got through the multiple choice okay, but he couldn't pass the sign recognition. I'm chauffeur now.

I took him over to Quincy in the afternoon to see Callie McAllister, his girlfriend. She's a nice old widow he met at the Quincy boat club some years back. She's quite tall. Facially she looks a little like William Bendix, the old actor. The two of them sit in Callie's parlor and watch talk shows. Yesterday the subject on "Oprah" was whether women should share their men with other women.

Uncle Rollie said, "How 'bout that, Callie. Would you share me?"

"I'd rather give you up altogether," she said.

After a couple hours, Uncle Rollie said, "Well, I better be goin' before it gets dark."

It's the most apathetic relationship I've ever seen, but he never misses a day.

When we got home, Uncle Rollie, Wendell, and I had a high-level strategic discussion in Wendell's mobile home kitchen.

We decided not to advertise the card in any newspapers. Wendell doesn't want to have to make any split-second decisions on whether to shoot at visitors or not. The way things are now, he says, he feels comfortable firing at any stranger that shows up. If we advertise the card, he might gun down a legitimate potential buyer.

I was interested in protecting the card. "Why don't you buy a safe deposit box downtown at the bank, put it in there and—?"

I stopped. Rollie and Wendell were both looking at me like I'd suggested putting the card on the table and eating off it.

"I'd as soon wipe my ass with it, Cooper," said Uncle Rollie. "Ailene Hansen's a teller down there; all she talks about is how she wants to go around the world. I'm not gonna drop the fare right in front of her." He blinked. "Reminds me, you got to watch out for Lloyd Wiemeier. He's jealous of your success."

"Why is it," I said, "that people here think everybody who works in Chicago is successful?"

"They think everybody who works *anywhere* is successful," said Uncle Rollie.

"Lloyd Wiemeier's got a job, doesn't he?"

"Oh, he's got some bullshit—what's his job, Wendell?"

"He's the mayor."

"That's right."

They told me Charlotte and Lloyd just got divorced, which explains why Charlotte said "Who cares?" at the 7-Eleven.

Uncle Rollie got tired before we decided anything, and he went home to bed. I went back and fell asleep early, too, with all the lights on, hoping to discourage intruders. If anybody broke in I didn't hear them. The Schulte card is in—well, I won't write that down.

"You're crazier than you look."

Mom was addressing Uncle Rollie and me collectively late this morning. We were standing in his yard, around my car.

The Dodge Colt is suffering. When I got up and looked out the kitchen window today, there were two goats from up the bluff standing on the hood. It looked like one of those Dali paintings. They were eating leaves off the tree I parked beside. This, in addition to the gunshot wound in the front left side, has sent my car into a decline.

"You're not doing him any favor by humoring him," Mom told me. She turned to Uncle Rollie, who was looking at the hole in my car. "What month is it, Roland?"

"Hmmm?" he said.

"Month. What month is it? What *year* is it? Whose *car* is that?"

"It's *Cooper's* goddamn car," said Uncle Rollie.

"Y'know, I wish you'd get off this subject of my memory. I'm looking *ahead*. Everybody's always sayin' don't live in the past. Well, I don't. I don't think about yesterday."

"And we know why."

"Just what in the hell concern is it of yours, Belle?" he said, walking around the car to approach her. "You oughtn't to worry about me. There's a whole world right outside town. Your talents are wasted here. You should be out there"—he gestured toward the Illinois side—"rectifying everything."

Mom's mouth tightened up.

"I don't deserve that," she said.

"Well, I don't deserve your help, Belle," he said. "I don't. I should be abandoned and left alone here. It's a fair punishment for me." He headed down the yard and toward the pier.

"He's going to check on his fish writing now," she said. "Last of the Bonapartes."

Uncle Rollie stopped and turned. "I heard that," he said. "That's another thing, Belle. How in the hell can you say I'm losing my mind? How could you tell? You *always* thought I was crazy."

"You've gone from bad to worse since you sold that tap. Now you've got all day to devote to your aberrations."

"Aberrations? How 'bout you? With your sky opening up and Jesus ridin' down on us like Tom Mix."

"The mockers," said Mom levelly, "are going to suffer."

"And you're gonna sit up in heaven while I burn in everlasting flame. Thanks a hell of a lot, Belle," said Uncle Rollie. Then he turned and went down to the pier.

"Pretty lively as far as I can see," I said.

"That's because you're here," Mom told me. "This is the most animated he's been in a year. He's trying to show you he can still function; when you leave he'll collapse. I saw him peeing on the river-bank, did I tell you that?"

"If they locked up everybody who ever peed in the river I don't believe there'd be a man left in town," I said.

"Dr. Starnes says it's a miracle with his drinking history that he can recognize his fingers and toes. He says he's going to get worse and worse until he's helpless."

I watched Uncle Rollie settling slowly into his pier chair.

"I don't see why he can't sit and look at his fish writing till then."

My mother gave me one of those parental looks that carry a lifetime's worth of unrealized expectations.

"You just can't face an unpleasant task," she said. "Your father couldn't either."

We were both silent for a moment, listening to the birds sing, recalling Dad. I was thinking about the last time we saw him, in his hospital room in Macomb, Illinois. He had cirrhosis; his face was yellow. He was drifting in and out. He seemed to want to tell me things, fatherly things. The last thing he told me was, "You can't run away from your problems." A little while later he died. Mom stood over him and said, "And what do you call *that?*"

After Mom left, washing her hands of me until the fish fry in Quincy tonight, Uncle Rollie took one of his naps and I walked downtown.

Front Street is just the same as it's always been except that it's two-thirds boarded up. It bakes in the sun for three blocks. The taverns provide the shade.

At one corner, beside a building with a Michelob sign hanging in front, I walked down a flight of stone steps and rapped on the door. Gordy O'Dell let me in. He was cleaning up.

Gordy's been running the basement tap since Uncle Rollie sold it after the big flood. Gordy is getting huge. It's like he acquired Uncle Rollie's old belly along with the bar. I asked him how he was doing.

"Well, all right. Back on our feet." He went in the back and came out with a case of Budweiser. "How's Chicago?"

"Oh, crowded, hot." People in LaPorte like to hear that it's unpleasant in Chicago. "When you gonna open?"

" 'Leven. Want a beer?"

"I'd like a Pepsi."

I complimented Gordy on what he'd done with the place since the flood, repairing it, putting in new bar stools. We played "Whatever happened to," talking about our Little League teammates of long ago.

After a few minutes I mentioned that somebody was breaking into my uncle's house lately. Gordy looked concerned.

"Black or white?"

"White, I believe."

"Well, shit, I know who it is."

That's an advantage of a small town; most of the mysteries are easily solved. Usually four or five people do just about everything.

"It's Billy Garner," said Gordy. "He's in here tradin' his baseball cards for drinks all the time; he's probably tryin' to steal Rollie's."

I brooded for a moment, and then I said, "Gordy, how do you know about Rollie's baseball card?"

"He *told* me. He told everybody in the bar."

I nodded.

"He says he's got one o' them rarities," Gordy went on.

"Well, he doesn't. *He's* a rarity, all right?"

"That's right enough," said Gordy. "That's what I figured. I love that old bastard, but you know he never makes any sense."

"Who's Billy Garner?"

"He moved here from Palmyra after you left. Hard times, ain't workin'..." Gordy shrugged. "Comes in here too much."

"And what was that about baseball cards?"

"He gives 'em to me, and I take 'em and price 'em and give him credit on his beer. I just do it for a favor, 'cause I like those old cards, you know? I'd

46

have thousands of 'em but my mother threw 'em out." Gordy shook his head at the memory. "I'll call you when he comes in—where are you, Belle's or Rollie's?"

"Rollie's. Is there a sheriff anymore?"

"There's Eldon, but he's sick. There's state police in Canton." Gordy wiped the bar. "Did he get anything? Is anything missing?"

"In that house you can't tell. He might've gotten away with some old sport sections or blankets or crackers or something. So long." I got up and headed for the door. Whenever I leave that tavern during the day, I feel like one of the mole people, going up the stairs into the light.

I walked back in the heat, by the river, past the wreck of Thorpe's flooded-out boathouse restaurant, and talked seriously to myself.

This situation calls for resource, I said. I need to be clever, like I used to be. My car won't run. If I start to Chicago in Uncle Rollie's creaky old pickup with the card in the glove box, I may not get there with it. Even if I do, I can't just stand on the corner with the card in my hand trying to sell it. I've got to protect it. I've got to know what it's worth so I don't get taken. First off, I've got to get out of LaPorte with it.

Mom is at least part right about Uncle Rollie. He's not thinking consistently. He'll spend an hour picking out the best place in the house to hide the card. Then he'll sit down across from me in a restaurant with the damn thing sticking out of his shirt pocket.

That was an eye-opener. We were at a booth in a Chuckwagon in Quincy before we went to see Callie yesterday. I thought the card was back at the house, guarded by Wendell. Then Uncle Rollie pulled out a pencil to figure out the check and the card fell out onto the table. This, after he'd spent a good portion of the previous night burying it in a silverware drawer.

I held up the plastic sleeve for him to see.

"Whatcha got here?" I asked.

He opened his mouth and peered at my hand. When he realized what I was holding—it took about five seconds—his eyes got buggy and he made a grab for it.

"Hey, gimme that, what the hell's wrong with you?" he said, looking around. "Get that outta sight. What's that doin' here?"

When I told him, he became embarrassed and fearful. He didn't remember picking it up or putting it in his pocket.

"You taking your pills?" I asked him. He's had some pills prescribed for reducing the swelling of the blood vessels in his head.

"Pills won't help what I got," he said.

It was the first time he'd really admitted that he had anything wrong with him. He seemed so lost all of a sudden, looking out the window at the street, that I didn't know what to do.

"Well, you know," I said finally, "they're making progress on Alzheimer's."

"I ain't got Alzheimer's!" he said, indignant. "I got *wet* brain if I got anything." He sat back. "They ain't makin' too much progress on *that*."

We sat for a while. I read the funnies. Uncle Rollie put the card back in his shirt pocket and looked at a story about the Cubs.

When we left I got a reminder of how far along I've come myself. Out in the parking lot, I couldn't find my car. I was looking all over. It wasn't there, of course.

"Where you goin'?" said Uncle Rollie. He was standing by his pickup. I'd walked right past it.

"You worry me, Cooper," he said. "You're supposed to be the brains."

CHAPTER FIVE

There was a big gray Mercury Sable in Uncle Rollie's yard when I got back from the tap. Beyond it, little Dillon Wiemeier, in a Cardinals cap, was running in erratic, darting patterns at the end of the road, snatching at the air. When I got closer I saw that he was trying to catch the autumn leaves as they blew down from the trees.

Charlotte was down by the pier with Uncle Rollie. She was wearing a gray jacket and had her hands in her pockets.

She's different—more assured than she used to be. She was self-conscious in high school. Now she moves very easily. Her smile is the same. Her eyes are as big as I remember. I don't know if they still have the little brown flecks in them; you have to be close up to tell.

Uncle Rollie was telling her how much better she looks now that she's left Lloyd, and congratulating her on how Dillon's turning out.

"You got a fine boy there, Charlotte," he said, while Dillon missed and then grabbed a leaf about a foot off the ground. "He don't have a mean, piggy face, like he might."

"You're sweet," said Charlotte.

"I meant, you know, after his daddy," said Uncle Rollie.

"He's a good boy," she said, watching him. "He's got no interest in anything useful, though. It's all video games and comics and . . ." She made a gesture to encompass what he was doing now.

When we went up the slope and sat on the porch to drink some pop, Uncle Rollie suddenly became shrewd and masterful.

"Listen here, Charlotte," he said. "Can you be trusted?"

"What with?" she asked.

"I need for Cooper to take a little package up to Chicago, only I ain't sure but what somebody might try to take it from him."

Charlotte looked from Uncle Rollie to me.

"Is this the baseball card collection?" she asked.

I sighed.

"How do *you* know about it?" said Uncle Rollie after his head had snapped back.

"You told Lloyd and me a couple months ago how you had some treasure in baseball cards that was going to cushion you in your old age."

"I told *Lloyd*? I don't even *speak* to Lloyd."

"You told me in his presence," said Charlotte.

"At one of the Sunday band concerts in Quincy."

"God*damn*," said Uncle Rollie.

"I hope you get the money," she said. "I think you should be allowed to stay here and write your fish poetry till the end of your days, even if it's a complete waste of time."

"I don't write it," said Uncle Rollie, with his teeth gritted a bit. "I edit it. The fish write it."

"Well, whatever," said Charlotte. She's intelligent but she's not alive to distinctions of a literary or journalistic nature. "What do you want me to do?"

He peered at her. "Cooper's car ain't ridin' too good. You say you're goin' up to Chicago pretty soon. How 'bout if he goes along with you?"

I was surprised. We hadn't discussed this.

"You can go up there," he continued, "and won't nobody know you've got this package, you see. They'll be watchin' for my truck or Cooper's car, not yours. And Cooper can scrunch down in the back till you get out of town."

He was completely taking over all of a sudden.

"Where'd *that* come from?" I asked. "Don't I even get consulted?"

He didn't answer because he had become mesmerized by the sight of Wendell Kendall walking toward us across the yard, back from Front Street with his day's bag of groceries. We all fell silent as he approached. Wendell moves so slowly and feebly that he holds your attention in a kind of suspense.

He reached us in about five minutes.

"Where's the fire, Wendell?" said Uncle Rollie.

Wendell looked down at me.

"Gordy says Billy Garner's down at the tap," he said.

When I got back to the basement tavern, there were six or seven customers in it—some of the more serious seekers of shade in LaPorte. Gordy, behind the bar, made a little gesture toward a man on one of the stools.

Some drinkers not only see things blurry, they *are* blurry. Billy Garner is a short, slender, fortyish guy with a muddy, smeared look to his face. He had on a dirty white T-shirt and jeans. He was summoning up some animation when I came in because he was mad at Gordy.

"I got a tab with you," he was saying.

Gordy shrugged. "You sure do."

"Whaddya mean by that?"

"You're behind."

"Bullshit, you got the Mathews, you got the Killebrew, you got every common up through '62."

Gordy glanced at me and then reached under his cash register to resolve the issue. "The last I got from you," he said, bringing out a clipboard, a shoe box, and a copy of *Baseball Card* magazine, "was September 14. A '59 Killebrew and '58 Mathews, like you say. That was for the previous billing period."

Garner was looking at Gordy's entries upside down, leaning over the bar. "What about the commons? We said the commons were worth three hundred dollars."

"Yeah, but if I *sell* 'em I'm lucky to get half that, ain't that right?" said Gordy. "Don't yank me now, Billy, we talked about this. I said half, you said fine."

"What are you sayin'?" said Billy Garner.

"I'm sayin' you're behind"—he looked for a spot on the clipboard, then spun it around so Garner could see—"a hundred forty-eight and you hit the wall with that beer."

Billy Garner turned away, saw me, and said, "What are *you* lookin' at?"

"I got the next one," I told Gordy.

"This is Cooper Zerbs, Billy," said Gordy.

I looked in Billy Garner's bloodshot brown eyes for some recognition of the name "Zerbs," and saw nothing.

"Even if he buys you one, Billy," Gordy went on, "you're a hundred and fifty down. I don't like to jump in your shit in front of people, but fair's fair and I been fair all summer, takin' cards. I wouldn't do it for anybody, y'understand what I'm sayin'?"

Billy Garner said nothing for a moment. Then he reached into his pants pocket and pulled out a little transparent plastic box.

"These are star cards," he said sullenly, and handed the box to Gordy, who opened it and took the cards out.

He thumbed them and said, "Well, these ain't gonna do it."

"Whaddya mean, that's Billy Pierce right there for starters. He was a great pitcher."

"In the book he's an eight-dollar pitcher," said Gordy.

"Listen," said Garner, his voice getting a little shaky, "the only reason I left my cards with you in the first place was because I thought you appreciated them."

"And you wanted some beers."

"When I get money I'm buyin' back the fuckin' cards, all right?"

"Meantime you owe the bar."

There was a pause while Billy Garner rubbed his face. Gordy whapped at the bar with a rag and said, "Shit." The whole scene was awkward, with me and the rest of the early drinkers hanging around. Billy Garner finally laughed, the way you do when you're embarrassed, and said, "Like it's a big deal."

He went into his shirt pocket this time, and came out with a hard plastic sleeve. In the sleeve was a '59 Bob Gibson.

There is nothing wrong with my memory where that card is concerned. I was too young to collect '59s, but I always wanted that card. My cousin Charlie was older and he had it when we were kids. But I deserved it more than Charlie did. He liked Lou Brock best. I liked Gibson best.

I think even a person who didn't give a damn about baseball cards—somebody who preferred antiques or paintings or books, or even a person who didn't care about anything—would be able to tell the '59 Gibson is a nice card. It's got a pink background. The picture is a circle in the middle, like all the '59s.

56

Gibson has a big fresh grin on his face. He's a hand-some, happy rookie, not the great, tough Bob Gibson yet.

Billy Garner's Gibson was still glossy. The corners were still sharp. It looked like a classic car. I had a strong impulse to grab it out of his hand and run.

"This card . . ." said Billy Garner.

Gordy looked in his magazine. ". . . is worth three hundred dollars, mint. Let's see it."

"Don't touch it. I'll hold it," said Billy Garner. He pinched the sleeve so it flared out and carefully extracted the card, holding it gently between thumb and middle finger. He turned it so Gordy could see the back.

Gordy nodded. "Awright," he announced. "Two hundred. That clears you and puts you fifty up. You can have these." He pushed the plastic box across the bar. "I'm doin' it because I like you and I appreciate a good pitcher."

He reached for the card and Garner pulled it back.

"You got to keep it in the sleeve," said Garner. "You don't touch it."

Gordy exhaled and looked at Garner from under his eyebrows. "I'm the only man in town who'd do this for you, Billy," he said. "Keep track o' your tone when you're talkin' to me." Then he waggled his fingers in a "gimme" gesture.

So I was there when Billy Garner gave up his '59 Gibson. You could see it was cutting him up.

Finally, handing it to Gordy, he laughed and shook his head.

"Piece o' cardboard," he said.

Well, I didn't want to bother him. When a guy's sitting there after doing something like that . . . you know he's feeling like a traitor to himself. That card had been a close childhood companion, more than likely. Probably his prize memento. And now he'd cut it loose. Would Citizen Kane have sold his sled for beers?

He would have if he'd been a drunk. I decided I'd make a little effort to help out my fellow man. I've had some experience with alcohol.

I waited until Gordy had walked away, down the bar, and then I said, "Y'know, I used to hammer that beer pretty good, too, but it finally wore me out. I feel better since I quit."

Billy Garner looked at me.

"You sure turned *me* around," he said. "You're a regular fuckin' movie of the week."

We exchanged stares for a moment and decided we'd never be pals.

"Okay," I said. "Somebody's been breakin' into my uncle's house out past the silo every night. Any idea who that might be?"

"How would I know?"

"I don't know. But if you happen to figure out who it is, tell him we're ready for him now, okay?"

"Why don't *you* tell him?"

"All right, then, dammit, we're ready for you

now." I was getting sore. You couldn't use any kind of indirect approach with this guy.

"Are you accusin' me of somethin' here?"

My head was getting that feeling of density again, like everything inside it was shrinking.

"Here's what I'm saying," I said. "And this is addressed to whoever is breaking into Rollie Zerbs's house." I raised my voice for the benefit of the room. "Wendell Kendall is on patrol. And Wendell Kendall will never be convicted by a jury of his peers."

I put five dollars on the bar and went out the door and back up the steps, blinded by the light again.

CHAPTER SIX

When I got back to Uncle Rollie's again, he and Charlotte and Wendell were pretty thick. They were sitting in Uncle Rollie's kitchen and he was frying jowl bacon for everybody. His face was flushed and his hair was standing up all over. Dillon was in the sitting room watching TV.

"Cooper," said Uncle Rollie, "Charlotte's goin' up there to Chicago. She'll take the card and you."

"If you got it all worked out, what do you need me for?" I said.

"Yeah, what do we need him for?" said Charlotte to Uncle Rollie.

"He's gonna sell it for me, get a good price, too. Don't come back here with less'n five thousand," he said to me.

The old man was getting way above himself. He was acting like the head of the allied forces.

"We don't know what it's worth," I told him.

"Call your boss back, maybe he can tell you," said Charlotte. She handed me a piece of paper. "He left his number in case you forgot it."

When I got through to Casey he said everything was fine at Neatly Chiseled Features.

"I talked to Mad Dog McClure," he said.

"Who is that, an old actor?"

"You're thinking of Mad *Doug* McClure. Mad *Dog* McClure is a collectibles dealer, he's got a big store up in Evanston. He says *if* it's really a Roberto's Schulte, and *if* it's near-mint, you could have something."

"What's it worth?"

"Mad Dog said he'd have to see it."

"He didn't put a figure on it?"

"No."

"What would you do, Casey?"

"I don't know. Look for a collector. Mad Dog's in a big card show this weekend, you could try that. Chicago's the place to peddle an old Cub card. We're still alive in the playoffs. 'Djou see the game last night?"

"Nope."

He gave me play-by-play on the last inning and a half and then he had to go.

While I was on the phone, Uncle Rollie asked me four times who I was talking to, and I told him four times.

"Here's what, Cooper," said Charlotte after I hung up. "Me and Dillon are going up to drop off my painting with the Mr. Green Genes restaurant people. Wendell has to work on your car anyway, so you come up with us tomorrow and I'll drop you off home. If you get your deal done Friday we'll drive back together, or you can come back to Quincy later on the train." She *ba-dumped* her hands on the kitchen table.

I blinked.

"Who thought all that up?"

"We put our heads together," said Charlotte.

"Where you goin' to put the card?" asked Wendell.

Uncle Rollie stared in front of him, as if he was thinking, "What card?"

"I'll put it in a book," I said, "and hold it on my lap. The only thing to watch out for is that it hasn't been in direct sunlight for eighty-five years."

"The card," said Uncle Rollie, having refocused, "goes in here." He held up his thermos. "Vacuum-sealed."

He wouldn't entertain any other suggestions, so we adjourned.

Charlotte started out the door after Dillon, then came back. I thought she wanted to say something to Uncle Rollie, but she walked past him, to me.

"Missed you, Coop," she said.

She still has the brown flecks in her eyes. I don't know where I thought they would have gone. She was cute when she was young but now she's beautiful.

Her hair and cheek brushed my face as she gave me a friendly hug. In order to keep it just friendly on my part I had to stand sideways. We hadn't touched in several years but my reaction to her was surprisingly prompt. I got it on contact. I couldn't have saluted much faster.

Trouble is there's no future in it. There's no future in *us*. I can see now that we wouldn't make a match anymore even if she were interested and I weren't with Irene.

I'm not one of these men who thinks he has to be smarter than the woman, but I do think the man ought to have something to say to her besides, "Huh?" I'd be deadweight for Charlotte now. She's become much more alert than me. A woman's mate should share the load, not *be* the load. It's bad enough she had to be with Lloyd for ten years.

So anyway, I took her on the hip, gave back a one-armed hug, and said, "Missed you, too." She looked at me funny. Probably wonders where I get all those bright remarks.

They had a big fish fry over at the Quincy boat club tonight, and of course Uncle Rollie declined to attend. He hasn't eaten a fish since he was thirty-five years old and got the calling. He doesn't condemn others for it; he just won't do it himself.

I went with Mom and ran into a few people from LaPorte—mainly Lloyd Wiemeier.

Lloyd is a tall, lanky guy with short hair, a gaunt face, and blue eyes set back in his head. I first began to dislike him when he and Charlotte got together. Before that I was indifferent. When we were kids we played together once in a while if our friends weren't available.

Tonight we spoke because we got our food at the same time. The long tables were out near the riverbank, and we wound up standing together with our paper plates. We agreed it was a nice night, and then Lloyd stabbed his catfish and said, "Hope this isn't one of your uncle's authors."

"Good one, Lloyd."

"Reason I bring it up," he went on, poking around for bones, "is I think your mother's got the right idea about old Rollie. He's best supervised, I think."

"That so?"

"Well, he's not too good for the town right now. You know how every year he's on the Quincy news. It's like he symbolizes LaPorte. Who wants to start a business in a town where the best-known citizen—lovable though he may be—"

"He's not so lovable," I said.

"Point is he makes us all look bad."

"I appreciate your taking an interest in my family's affairs, Lloyd. What went wrong with you and Charlotte?"

He tightened up. "I don't see that's any of your business," he said.

"I don't see how my uncle's any of yours."

"He's a concern to me as the mayor."

"All right, you and Charlotte are a concern to me as a friend."

"I don't think of you as a friend, Cooper."

"Well, I don't think of you as a mayor, Lloyd."

A typical get-together for Lloyd and me. We didn't yell "Are too" and "Am not" and start to wrestle, but that was mostly because my mother came up to us at this point.

Lloyd said, "Belle, how are you?"

"I'm fine," she said. "You look blotchy, Lloyd. Are you eating? If you don't eat enough you hallucinate."

"I'd better get some more, then," he said, and moved off.

Mom said to me, "That boy grew up in height only. He cheated on Charlotte, you know. She should have left him years ago. She only married him in the first place on the rebound from you."

"On the *run* from me."

"She was crazy about you, and she was perfect for you. You knew better, though, didn't you? Still living with that little snip?"

"If you mean Irene," I said austerely, "I have no idea."

It seemed a good time and place to break the latest news to Mom. She'll never make a scene in public.

"I'm going up to Chicago with Charlotte tomorrow," I began.

Her eyes widened.

"You surprise me, Cooper," she murmured.

"It's not for anything you're going to approve of," I said.

"I may surprise *you* on that score."

"She's going up to drop off her painting for Mr. Green Genes. I'm going up to sell a baseball card for Uncle Rollie so he can have some money to stay home with."

There was a longish silence between us. She nodded, more to herself than to me. Then she took her paper plate over to a trash barrel, dumped it, and started for her car. I followed along.

"It's not like he's hurting anybody with his fish poetry. He even uses plastic hooks."

"Oh, *well*," she said.

"A man ought to be able to pursue his hobby," I argued, "even if it's not real meaningful. Look at these people who get in the Guinness book because they lived inside a piano for a month."

Mom kept walking.

"And how crazy is he, anyway? He says the fish are writing the stuff. Well, they are, aren't they? Maybe he's right about them. Maybe they're going to give investment advice."

She wouldn't respond, all the way home. She's not speaking to me now.

It's ten o'clock and I'm turning in—it's going to be an early day. Uncle Rollie went to bed soon after I got back. First we put Wildfire Schulte, encased in his plastic sleeve, into the thermos and put the thermos away.

I went up a minute ago to check on Uncle Rollie. He was sacked out with his mouth open, his habitual way of sleeping. I don't know why he doesn't have a sore throat all the time.

I turned out the bedside lamp and started out. Behind me, he said, "I was wrong to sell the tap. Didn't think I was up to fixing it after the flood, but . . . I don't hardly get any company anymore."

I stood in the doorway, uncertain what to say. "Well, there's Wendell," I said finally.

"Yeah, there sure is Wendell." He paused before going on. "Appreciate what you're doin', Cooper. Hope I helped you, too, gettin' you back together with Charlotte. She's under your spell, boy."

"Uh-huh."

"Don't make my error. I always thought I could do better."

He was silent again for a few moments.

"You know," he said, "in my dreams I can run. Climb things. I talk to girls I haven't seen for forty, fifty years. You can't believe it."

He wished me good night and turned over, and I went back downstairs.

CHAPTER
SEVEN

The clock radio in the sitting room woke me at 4 a.m. I could hear Uncle Rollie shuffling around upstairs. I took a shower, and Charlotte drove up with Dillon at 4:30, calling across the yard at Wendell not to shoot. Uncle Rollie walked with me through the dark to her car and handed me the thermos. He supervised me while I slid it under the passenger seat. Then I straightened up and we shook hands.

"Cooper," he said, "I'll never forget this."

I was touched. Brave words, I thought.

Charlotte said she wanted to drive the first leg, even though she looked a little tired and washed-out. She'd stayed up to watch an old movie with Cary Grant and Deborah Kerr.

"A sad one," she said as we came off the gravel out onto Route 5.

"Did you cry?" I asked.

"Oh, God."

Dillon was stretched out asleep in back with Charlotte's painting. It showed a farmhouse, kids in a field picking corn, a woman with a basket of tomatoes in the foreground. It had a bright, yellow-green, healthy look to it.

"The Mr. Green Genes people want to stress the field instead of the laboratory," Charlotte said.

"You've progressed since that portrait of me," I said.

She laughed. "I was just starting then."

"I still have it. Wherever I move, I keep it in the closet."

"It's a subtle difference in the eyes. I tried to do a lively expression and you came out insane instead."

I glanced back at Dillon.

"So you and Lloyd are done?"

She took a deep breath.

"Well, we weren't a great romance, but we were a marriage and I would've stuck by that. He didn't." She yawned.

She caught me looking at her and said, "Listen, I *did* my crying about that. Women cry *during* the relationship."

I nodded. "It's the man's job to cry after."

"How's your head?" she asked after about a mile. "Your mom said you got a concussion saving Irene's life."

I coughed.

"Didn't happen?" she asked.

"Well . . ."

It wasn't a matter of deciding whether to tell her

or not. It was a question of recall. As the last event
of my unimpaired life, it's fairly clear up to a point,
and then it skips. I remember it up to where Big Stan
Cornell hit me.

Big Stan is head of the production department at
Neatly Chiseled Features. He used to go with Irene,
who works downstairs in the credit union, but she
left him a year ago.

Stan got to brooding after they broke up and
found he couldn't stand it. He asked Irene to come
back and said he'd talk to her as well as to the Bulls,
Bears, Cubs, and Sox on TV. But she wouldn't.

I had a party for some people from the office at
my apartment one night last winter and Irene came
alone. Stan came later with a load on, and they got
into an argument out on the sidewalk. I went outside
in time to see him whack her open-handed on the side
of the head.

I stepped between them because I was the host,
but I didn't feel good about it. If Irene had gotten up
onto my shoulders, we would have been as tall as
Stan.

I remember him swaying on his heels, all bleary
and anguished. He looked like the kind of guy you
read about in the paper who shoots his ex-girlfriend
and whoever's with her and then kills himself, and
they quote a male acquaintance saying, "I guess he
just loved her too much."

"If you don't get outta my way," he said, "I'm
gonna knock your head through the side o' the
fuckin' building."

I'll never forget that statement. I've forgotten a number of things since, though, because the big dumb donkey ended up *trying* to knock my head through the side of the building.

I remember I said, "There's no excuse for hitting a woman, Stan."

So often, after the event, we think of what we should have said. In this case what I should have said was that Stan oughtn't to hit anyone at all.

Anyway, he punched me; I ducked a little bit and he got me on the forehead. I staggered back into the concrete windowsill that jutted out from the wall of my building and I hit my head on that.

For the rest of the story that night I have to depend on Irene's version, because mine is now over.

Irene says I didn't fall or pass out. I got incensed at Stan. I said, "Now you've done it. You've fractured my skull." I took a swing at him and hit him, a blow I'm sure he has yet to feel.

Stan grabbed for Irene but missed her, and some other people from the party came outside. Then Stan said something like, "Oh, I don't care, who cares, I don't care. I don't give a damn." And he got in his car and drove off. Irene says I followed him to the car and banged on the roof, yelling, "What about my *head*? Who's going to pay for my *head*?" And after he left, I took Irene back inside and told her she should stay at my place until Stan got counseling.

The next thing *I* recall is her clothes in my bedroom and pictures of kittens hanging on the walls.

That's what I feel bad about. I started up with

her under false colors. That wasn't me. I don't swing on huge drunken acquaintances and carry their ex-girlfriends off to my apartment. Not when I'm conscious. But as it turned out, the segment of our relationship that I don't remember is the only part Irene liked.

When I finished the story, Charlotte said, "You're different than you used to be."

"Yeah, I've had about half my brains dislodged."

"Is that what it is? Used to be nothing in LaPorte was good enough for you. You had to get out of town and do things. You don't seem so ambitious now."

"Well, I found a little spot for myself and now I'm trying to keep it."

"And you're satisfied with that?"

"Oh . . . you accommodate yourself to partial satisfactions. Comes a time you decide they're probably not going to add you to Mount Rushmore."

We played the radio and rolled through some of those Illinois towns you never stop in. In two hours we made Havana, where I usually stop for a bite, and parked next to a Golden Corral. I'd been watching in the rearview, and nobody was following us.

I decided to take the thermos into the restaurant with us. I unscrewed the top to look in and make sure the card hadn't gotten into some odd position.

It wasn't there.

As I held the thermos up like a kaleidoscope and stupidly rotated it—there didn't seem to be any nooks or corners inside—I was struck again by the reflection that my mind was just a condensed version of what it should be, that I had apparently achieved eighty years' worth of mental decay in less than half the time.

"Did you put it somewhere else?" asked Charlotte.

"How would *I* know?"

We looked in the glove box and on the floor under the dash. We looked under both car seats. We looked out on the pavement. We woke up Dillon to ask him if he'd taken it in his sleep.

"Where's the last place you saw it?" Charlotte asked me.

"In the thermos."

"When?"

"Uncle Rollie gave it to me this morning."

"Gave you what?"

"The *thermos*."

"Was the *card* in the thermos?"

"*Yes*." I looked at her. "I don't know."

"When was the last time you saw the card?"

I exhaled. "I don't *know*."

"When was the last time you *remember* seeing the card?"

I did my best to concentrate.

"You look like Jerry Lewis trying to think," Charlotte said.

"I can't picture it this morning, I can only see it last night."

"Maybe your uncle took it out."

"Well, that's dumb. Why would he do that?"

I thought about it. Then I ran around behind the

car and hopped in the driver's side, saying, "God, I hope so. I hope it's him and not me."

It was noon by the time we got back to LaPorte and pulled into Uncle Rollie's yard. I yelled to Wendell so he'd know it was us. Uncle Rollie's truck wasn't there.

Wendell came down his three steps, unarmed, and inched toward us as we got out of the car.

"Where's Uncle Rollie?" I hollered.

"He left." Wendell started across his yard toward his birdbath. He's always checking the water level in his birdbath.

"Wendell, I lost the card, it's not in the thermos."

"You didn't lose it. He wrote you a note."

"What?"

"There's a note in his kitchen," said Wendell.

Uncle Rollie's note said:

Dear Cooper:
    I decided to take the _____ up myself. I got afraid you might lose it. You had trouble remembering about your car yesterday and some other things.
    Please check the paper and the bait.
Your Uncle R.

"Well," I said, "I didn't make the cut. I got replaced by the fish editor."

I crumpled the note and threw it sidearm into the oven, which was open—and, of course, on. The note bounced back out onto the floor and Charlotte picked it up, uncrumpled it, and read it while I walked around the kitchen, mad.

"*I* have trouble remembering?" I said. "What's he doing here, preheating? He left the door unlocked, he leaves the note lying out on the table. He's going to fool everybody by leaving a blank instead of the word 'card.' " I looked out the window at the river. " 'Check the paper and the bait.' He's special, don't you think? Maybe someday they'll name a delusion after him."

"Maybe he sent us out first," said Charlotte, "so if anyone was watching they'd follow us and then he could go."

"You mean we were *decoys*?"

"My dad," said Charlotte, "up until his last year, had little patches where he could be sharp and mean as anything."

Out the window, Dillon was catching leaves in the breeze again. Wendell was still on his way to his birdbath.

"I used to wonder," I said, "how middle-aged people could talk so cold about putting their elders away. I mean, the middle-aged people are gonna be old in five minutes themselves. They should show more respect for their imminent condition. But now I've got to think Mom's onto something. He should have a rope around his waist with one end tied to that tree out there."

* * *

The old Royal typewriter sat at the end of the pier as always, riding up and down slightly.

I went out to the end and squatted to look at the paper. But all that the fish had written—I'm thinking like him now—all that the fish had *typed* was "fon." "F-O-N." The big dummies.

I rebaited the hooks and we drove north again.

CHAPTER EIGHT

We had a little inspiration about where he might be, but it didn't pan out. He hadn't gone to his girlfriend Callie's in Quincy. She was watching Oprah by herself.

So we rode upstate again, settling in to watch both sides of the road for 306 miles in case Uncle Rollie had actually gone in the direction he intended. It was hot. I was exasperated and worried. Charlotte finally asked me to turn the radio off because I was punching the buttons like a typist.

"Maybe you're right," I said. "Maybe he's a mastermind. He makes these transparent attempts at secrecy, which he undermines by telling everybody the secret. Then he sends us out to be followed and runs down the left sideline into the end zone all by himself." I didn't believe it, though. I thought it more likely that he forgot his own plan and went off the field altogether, to Keokuk or New Orleans or a stranger's house.

If Charlotte hadn't been with me I'd've been more upset than I was. Her prediction that we'd catch up to him was soothing. The conversation itself was a novelty for me. I'd forgotten you could talk in a car. When Irene and I drive together we depend upon the radio.

I can't recall much of what Charlotte and I said. Seems whatever you say or think in a car gets left in it when you get out, for some reason. I know she told me about how she lost Dillon once at a swap meet.

"For an hour. My temperature went up to one hundred and fifty. I ran around hollering. There's all these boys now named D-Y-L-A-N, and I kept finding the wrong boy. Turned out he was looking at a crossbow in the back of a pickup. He was sitting in the truck, I couldn't see him."

"What'd you do when you found him?"

"Well, he's got one ear sticks out further than the other one now."

Dillon snickered in the backseat.

I was glad she didn't disparage my judgment when we got behind a slow car on the two-lane section between Quincy and Havana. You hate to have somebody saying, "Why don't you pass him?" and then when you move out, screaming, "NOTNOW-NOTNOWNOTNOW!" and throwing themselves around the passenger seat. I don't like it when Mom does it and I know other drivers hate it when I do it.

About a mile outside a small cluster of buildings

called Guthrie, Illinois, we saw Uncle Rollie's pickup, pulled over on a cornfield shoulder. I stopped behind it and we all got out.

I walked up slowly, trying to prepare myself for the sight of him keeled over, but he wasn't there. My address was taped to the steering wheel.

We left the truck where it was and drove on into Guthrie, Pop. 1332. A hundred yards past the sign we saw Uncle Rollie standing outside a gas station, talking to an attendant or mechanic and a potbellied older man. Uncle Rollie was showing them something in his hand.

"He's trading the card for a tow," I said.

As we pulled up to him and got out, I heard him proclaim, "Every sonofabitchin' pump in the place, that's what."

He looked at me with a little flicker of confusion, then nodded. He was sweaty and puffing some.

"Hi, Uncle Rollie," I said.

"These boys think I'm no use because I don't have a Visa," he said. "I been telling 'em I can buy this entire building and occupants with this right here."

He held up the Schulte. It was still intact in its sleeve.

I looked at the attendant and shook my head. He and his pal, however, were too intrigued by the card to pay any attention to me.

"How much is it worth?" asked the older guy.

"I *told* you," Uncle Rollie said patiently, "it's the only one there is."

The Guthrie boys kept looking at it. I didn't like the situation. I'd never stopped in Guthrie before. For all I knew it could be one of those hell towns. These guys could be in a chain saw cult. The older man seemed harmless enough, but the attendant had a reptile tattoo on his right arm and one of those skinny, oily, snaggletoothed faces.

"He's always trying to pay for things with that old card," I said. I leaned forward to mutter at the Guthrie boys, "He thinks his underwear's made of spun gold."

"He seems all right to me," said the attendant.

Charlotte caught my eye at this point and mouthed the word "Poetry." I made her do it again, then got it.

"Well, you know you got something a lot more valuable than that card, Uncle Rollie," I said, reaching in his shirt pocket. I unfolded a piece of paper and showed it to the Guthrie boys. "Know what this is?"

"Oh, they don't care about that," said Uncle Rollie.

"Now just a minute. Take a look at this."

The Guthrie boys peered at it suspiciously. It was one of the later ones, transcribed in Uncle Rollie's scrawl. Went something like, "bones of a diesel tailor/ my seldom hair flew by."

"That's a poem. Know who wrote it?" I nudged Uncle Rollie. "Tell 'em."

He was reluctant. "People don't believe it," he muttered.

"Nobody's ever gonna appreciate this stuff if you don't tell 'em who wrote it."

Uncle Rollie cleared his throat.

"Fish wrote that," he said. "Mississippi fish. Missouri side. Took 'em about six months. A fish," he explained, "I don't care what kind, can't spell for shit. You have to cross out the errors. Unless you got till infinity, like they say to do with monkeys."

Whatever interest the Guthrie boys had had in Uncle Rollie and the card completely dissipated by the end of this speech.

"Has he really got a truck?" the attendant asked me.

While the attendant drove off to tow the pickup into town, I took it upon myself to lecture my uncle.

"One, you're not supposed to drive. Second, I'm supposed to have the card. And C, what the hell were you showing it to these guys for? They're not family. They mighta cut your head off." I held out my hand in my version of Gordy O'Dell's "gimme" gesture.

He compressed his lips defiantly and put the card back in his shirt pocket.

"Daddy gave it to me, not you," he said. "He gave you that money, coulda used it for the tap."

I didn't fully follow this. He seemed to have me confused with my father.

"I'm Cooper."

His head snapped back, then he shook it impatiently.

"I know that," he said, and looked around. "Where are we?"

"We're on our way to Chicago," said Charlotte.

She told him we were all going up in her car. This delighted him.

"I wouldn't mind sitting down," he said. "I wouldn't mind some air-conditioning."

We bought Uncle Rollie a grape soda and sat him on a bench in the shade until the attendant returned with the truck, which had a hole blown in its radiator. I paid for the tow and said we'd be back in a day or two, and we all got into Charlotte's wagon—me and Charlotte in the front and Uncle Rollie and Dillon in the back. The old man grunted with fatigue and relief as he sank onto the backseat.

"More like it," he said. He smiled affably at Dillon. "Where we goin'?"

We got to the North Side at nine at night. Uncle Rollie was impressed with how brightly lit Chicago was; much more so, he said, than when he lived there as a boy.

I live in a ground-floor apartment on Janssen, about eight blocks west of Wrigley Field. Charlotte wasn't going to come in—said she'd just go back out to the Holiday Inn on Ogden Avenue. But Dillon wanted to see some of the original comic strips from work, and there was no point her sitting out in the car alone. So we all trooped in to give Irene a treat.

She wasn't there. The place was clean, all picked up, and uninhabited. I thought I'd forgotten to call ahead, but my voice was on the answering machine. To my surprise, Irene had also left a message. Her voice came into the room briskly, after mine.

"Cooper, this is Irene. *Irene*. Play the tape in the VCR."

I turned the TV on while Uncle Rollie and Dillon looked at the framed strips on the walls. Charlotte stood beside me in the living room and watched it while I did.

The tape starred Irene. It showed her in the bedroom, packing her stuff.

"As you can see, Cooper," she said to the camera, "I'm leaving. Stan's made a change in his life and I think it's the real thing." She moved forward, out of the frame, which wandered around a bit and then revealed Big Stan himself, looking embarrassed.

"Hi, Cooper," he said. "You're probably thinking this is chickenshit, me in your crib when you're not here."

Irene's voice said, "You don't have to apologize for that. I told you to come over and help me."

Stan scratched his cheek and continued: "I want to make amends for what I did to you that night. I don't even remember doing it." He fished in a pants pocket. "I got a six-month sobriety chip now. Big deal, huh?" He brought it out and held it up briefly. "It's a big deal for me, anyway. I know it doesn't mean shit to you, but I'll do whatever I can to . . . well, make amends. I've got a lot of amends to make to you and Irene."

"Enough amends, Stan," said Irene, and switched places with him again.

The camera followed her into the kitchen. She went through some logistical stuff about why she was taking this and that utensil. She hesitated over the toaster and decided to leave it, although she'd bought it. Then she took a deep breath and shivered.

"Cooper, I'm fond of you," she said, very firmly, "but I'd be going even without Stan. I won't stay with a man who keeps forgetting *who I AM*." She paused, exhaled, and said, "I guess it's not your fault. Anyway I thought I'd tell you this way instead of just leaving a note. I'll always appreciate what you did. I still like you. Or at least, I like you more now that I'm leaving. And as far as the stuff I said about you being a lump and wasting your life away, you can go ahead and forget that. Too." She looked past the camera and said, "Okay, that's it."

The tape went to snow. My face was pretty hot. It was the first time I'd ever been critiqued on TV. And Charlotte was standing right there. The show had held her, all the way through.

"Wow. A Dear John videotape," she said. "Are you all right? You look goggle-eyed."

"So do you."

"Well, I thought she wanted you to watch a movie. I didn't expect it. How do you feel?" she asked.

I was moving past embarrassment toward something calmer and not unpleasant. I waited for that feeling you get sometimes when somebody jilts

86

you, where you suddenly can't take it. But it wasn't happening. There was nothing wrong with Irene, but the only thing she and I really had in common was that Stan had whacked us both in the head.

She loved Stan, anyway. She talked about him a third of the time even when she was determined never to see him again.

And here was Charlotte, after all. All day, when I hadn't been worrying about Uncle Rollie, I'd been thinking strange and foreign thoughts: thoughts about improving myself, about making more money, about quitting my job and doing something more worthy of admiration; becoming, perhaps, a National Geographic photographer. It was because of Charlotte. Irene's opinion of me glanced off, but Charlotte's was vital. All day long I'd been looking for intelligent things to say. I hadn't said any, but the point was I'd been searching. With Irene I didn't do that. All day I'd been aware of Charlotte's proximity, exactly how much space there was between us. When Charlotte stands next to you, half your mind is taken up with noticing that she's there. You get self-conscious. When we'd stopped for sandwiches in Bloomington I'd skipped the barbecue burger because of how the sauce might look on me.

I looked into the brown flecks, trying to remember what she'd asked me. There was a knock on the hall door. Dillon was next to it and opened it. Billy Garner walked in with a rifle.

It made the whole living room shrink.

*   *   *

Billy looked ill. He came in fast but he jumped spasmodically when he got inside, thinking there was something or someone coming up to him on his left. There wasn't.

Charlotte was outraged. She recognized Billy, and didn't seem to think much of him. She made a comment about how inappropriate and intrusive it was to bring a rifle into a four-room flat.

"My *boy's* in here," she concluded.

"I want that card," said Billy, blinking rapidly. His breathing was ragged. He held the gun up and pointed it at us, from the hip.

I was scared. I didn't know whether he'd shoot it on purpose or from the shakes, but I thought he was going to shoot it.

This was worse than the confrontation with Big Stan. I've disliked rifles, anyway, ever since I watched my Grampa Tyke shoot a squirrel out of one of his walnut trees when I was five or so. The squirrel landed at my feet with one eye gone and the other bulging out at me, demanding an explanation.

I stepped in front of Charlotte, proving to myself that my feelings for her were deep indeed. I don't think I would have stepped in front of anyone else. I admit I didn't *leap* in front of her.

Dillon walked silently over to his mother. She grabbed him by the upper arm and held him behind her, so we were in a line of three. Uncle Rollie was in the kitchen doorway, to our left and behind us, looking quizzically at Billy.

"I want that card," Billy repeated. "Where is it?"

Uncle Rollie seemed to think that was a pretty good question. His hand went into his shirt pocket and came out with nothing but fish poetry.

"I don't know," he said, looking from his notes to me.

I stared at him. I felt in my pockets.

"*Where is it?*" Billy was pale and sweaty and looked as scared as us.

I thought, well, hell. He could torture us and it wouldn't make any difference.

"Billy," I said, "you might have to come back." I looked at Charlotte. "Did we give it to you?"

He didn't believe us.

"Don't BULLSHIT me!" Billy was practically wailing. "I want it NOW!"

"I wouldn't give the time of day to somebody talked like that," said Charlotte.

"I know you," said Uncle Rollie, squinting at him. "Who are you?"

"He's a little walking hissy-fit," said Charlotte. "He's a wuss. I hope you're proud of yourself, Billy."

I murmured to her like Edgar Bergen, while we both faced the rifle.

"Why are we challenging his manhood?" I asked.

"I want the CARD!" he yelled, and almost sobbed. "I don't want to hurt anybody, but you better give it to me. I don't feel good and I'm gettin' mad."

"I know it sounds strange," I told him, "but we don't know what we did with it. We have to look for it. It might be in the car."

While I was telling him this, Big Stan Cornell

walked in the open door behind him. I was so much gladder to see Stan than I've ever been that it must have registered on my face.

Billy turned. Big Stan saw the rifle barrel swinging toward him and blocked it with his hand. Billy looked up at him and kind of whimpered. Then he jerked the trigger.

He just obliterated the middle of the second shelf of my bookcase, where I had the only remaining photograph of Monk, my boyhood dog. That was a memento. I think about it now and I get madder and madder. Billy Garner seemed to believe he could go through the Zerbs family dwellings like Sherman's army.

He now began fighting for breath and collapsed to his knees, letting go of the rifle. Billy did this on his own; nobody was doing anything to him. Big Stan held the gun and looked down.

"Hunh . . . hunh . . ." said Billy.

"What's the matter?" asked Big Stan.

"Oh, God . . . heart attack . . . I'm getting shocks inside my chest."

"I'll give you a heart attack, you little weevil," said Charlotte, walking past me to go stand over him. "Scare my kid? Here, have some CPR, Billy." She began pounding at his chest and face. Billy squirmed and wriggled on the floor, his arms up and slapping back up at her. Stan watched, bemused, as I came over and pulled Charlotte up and away.

"This fella a drinker?" Stan asked.

"He's a little piece of shit," said Charlotte.

"Well, but he drinks a lot?"

"Can't you smell him?"

"I ain't had a drink," moaned Billy. "I took a vitamin."

"There's your problem," said Charlotte contemptuously.

Stan squatted down beside Billy, who was gulping.

"How you doin' there, fella?"

Billy took a deep breath. "Okay. Not so good."

"His name's Billy?" Stan asked. "Billy, you need a drink?"

"Yeah. Yeah."

Stan straightened up.

"He's kind of seized up. He could use a beer and then about ninety meetings in ninety days, but that's up to him."

I bent over to talk to Billy.

"Hey, Billy, you been breaking into Uncle Rollie's house, ain'tcha?" He nodded, resting his cheek on the hardwood. "You gonna come after us anymore?" He shook his head. "Look at me." Billy looked up at me.

"I won't," he said.

I looked at Uncle Rollie.

"You want him arrested?"

Uncle Rollie looked down at Billy.

"Oh, hell. He's a liquor bum is all."

"Well, he doesn't look well enough to kick out in the street and I'm not nice enough to let him stay."

"How about if I take him with me?" offered

Stan. "I'm on my way to a meeting. That can't kill him. If he has a problem we'll go to emergency." Stan helped Billy up to a chair, where Billy slumped bonelessly. Then Stan stood there looking uncomfortable.

"You saw the tape?" he asked me.

I nodded.

"I came back for Irene's Diane Schuur CD. She said it was over here in the . . ." He went and got it, and turned. "Listen, Cooper. I've got to make amends to you for what I did. It's part of my program."

"Oh, forget about it, Stan. I pretty much have."

"Well, I gotta do something. It's been eating me up ever since I got sober."

"How about you take Billy out of here and we call everything even."

Stan looked down at Billy, who was well into the sweats.

"That's part of my program, too," he said. "Okay. We're not even, though. I know it."

"How's she doing?" I asked as he lifted Billy to his feet and started out.

"She's okay," he said, nodding solemnly. "She's okay."

"You stay with it, Stan," I said. "Or I might have to get rough with you again."

He took Billy out, without his rifle. And we commenced turning the apartment over, looking for the card. Dillon finally found it tucked in the *TV Guide*, where Uncle Rollie had put it as a bookmark, and Uncle Rollie pocketed it again.

We've got to be smarter about this.

CHAPTER NINE

Charlotte was worn-out by the time we found the card, and I was able to persuade her to forego the Holiday Inn. She and Dillon stayed overnight in the bedroom while Uncle Rollie and I slept in the living room, him on the couch and me on the floor.

In the morning I bustled around expansively as the host, making cheese omelets for everyone, with cereal and juice. Uncle Rollie was unsure of where he was but in good spirits, enjoying the company. Charlotte liked being waited on. She wore a turquoise robe and looked good sleepy. Some women look almost as bad as men waking up; they shock you. Charlotte wears hardly any makeup and consequently she doesn't look all washed-out when it's off.

Dillon wanted to rate how scared everybody had been last night when Billy came in. Whether, for instance, I'd been scareder than Uncle Rollie, and his mom had been scareder than me. My private opinion is that I had everyone else beat by two shits and a palpitation. Charlotte told Dillon it wasn't necessary to be afraid of Billy Garner.

The Cubs were now down three games to two in the playoffs with Los Angeles, and the *Times* sports section contained the obligatory reference to Cub history. Everyone in Chicago—*everyone*—knows that the Cubs haven't won the pennant since 1945. And most people know that the Cubs haven't won the World Series since 1908. Pretty soon they'll be tracking down the last surviving person who was alive when they did it, like they did with drummer boys from the Civil War.

There was an ad in the paper for the card show, which was at the downtown convention center. I had a one o'clock appointment at my doctor's for a progress report on my brain, and Charlotte was due to see the Mr. Green Genes people at 1:30. We decided we'd all go to the card show before splitting up.

Our argument over who would hold the card was short.

"It's mine," said Uncle Rollie.

"You keep forgetting where you put it," I said. "It's safer with me."

"It's been with me this long," said Uncle Rollie. "I'll watch over it and you can watch over me."

Charlotte had come up from LaPorte in jeans with dried paint on them. She now went back into the bedroom for forty-five minutes and came out in a flowered blouse and boots and something she called a crinkle skirt that she'd purposely brought up stuffed

94

in a nylon stocking. Most of her hair was up in a comb, with the rest hanging down in strands. She looked scrubbed, fresh, and sunny.

"I'm trying for artistic, but not slobby," she said, turning.

"You look great, Mom," said Dillon.

"Well, I'm not going up on the wall, but what the heck," she said. "I'll match the painting."

She was prepared to storm the city. She had become so brave. In our youth Charlotte would have interviewed in Transylvania as soon as Chicago. Back then she had a country shyness of this city that you find in some LaPorters. Not quite a phobia, but a pretty strong disinclination to come up here. Down to St. Louis maybe, up to Chicago never. It seems too big and rough and accelerated. They see it on the news and that's sufficient. And Charlotte had this feeling to an advanced degree. The night she realized I truly meant to leave home and live here someday, we had an argument and we couldn't get over it.

Now, I couldn't see a trace of that old timidity. She was all energy, determination, and motion. I was proud of her and sorry for myself. It seemed like we were always out of step; one of us was going while the other was stopped.

It was crisp outside, so we all wore jackets, except Uncle Rollie, who had come up without one. I gave him my overcoat to wear. He looked lost in it, but he liked the deep pockets.

*   *   *

The convention center was just north of the Loop, off Kinzie. It was five dollars to get in except for Dillon, who cost three. The flyer said Willie McCovey would be there to sign autographs in the afternoon.

It also said this was the big show of the year in the Midwest, and as we went into this indoor hangar called Hall C, I believed it. They had upwards of four hundred tables covering the floor. It wasn't just cards; they had bats and balls, uniforms and posters. And of course it wasn't just baseball; there was plenty of basketball and football stuff, and some hockey. There were comic books. There were live, in-person cheerleaders posing for pictures with customers. There were even centerfold cards, and cards of old TV shows.

But mostly there was all the baseball you could do with. There must have been at least one of every card a kid ever put in a shoe box. They were in stacks and rows and bins and under glass, laid out like blooms at Versailles. They were in plastic sleeves and Lucite holders, gazed at and haggled over. Over in a corner there was an armed guard in front of a glass booth featuring the 1910 Honus Wagner, the one McNall and Gretzky bought for $451,000. Of course, some people say they paid too much.

There were a couple ex-major leaguers at one end of the floor signing autographs already. I recognized Davy Tremayne, who used to play for and manage St. Louis. In another corner a dealer was holding an informal auction between two customers for a 1955

Roberto Clemente rookie card with a crease in it.

There were several slick displays by the modern card companies. Lots of dealers.

We walked up a few aisles and stopped at the display for Mad Dog McClure's store in Evanston. He had a fine selection of cards from the '50s and '60s under glass. The cards were in remarkable condition. They were actually shiny. I couldn't imagine what kid could ever have owned those cards. He must never have touched them except with tweezers.

Mantle, Maris, Aaron, Banks, Koufax . . . and over in a stack of sleeves on the side, the obscure players: Whammy Douglas, Vic Roznovsky, Bald Bobby Malkmus, Eli Grba . . . the childhood memories of the middle-aged man.

Charlotte said, "Look at all the grown-ups."

It was true. There were a lot of people my age or older. Fathers with sons, and even more solitary guys walking around. I don't recall many adults paying attention to baseball cards when I was a kid.

We were standing in front of Mad Dog Mc-Clure's booth when Charlotte made her comment about the grown-ups, and Mad Dog himself was standing right there—we could tell because there was a catalogue on his table with his picture on it. He was a tall, skinny, melancholy-looking guy, not at all the kind of used-car salesman type you'd take him to be from his name.

"Some of these prices seem kind of steep," I said to him, looking down at a 1961 Mickey Mantle All-

Star card with a $400 sticker on it. "How much can cardboard be worth?"

"I don't know," said Mad Dog McClure. "How much are your memories worth?"

He had me there; I'm vulnerable on that point. We Zerbses value our memories since we have so few. And I could see that for a man of a certain age, baseball cards could be the equivalent of those biscuits Proust encountered as an adult that evoked his entire childhood.

In Illinois and Missouri, for the last century or so, fan affiliation has been handed down from generation to generation. Most kids have grown up rooting for the ball team their father and grandfather rooted for. Baseball's history is intertwined with the history of all of us who grew up that way.

A baseball card of, say, Ron Santo calls up images that radiate out from Santo himself to include his teammates, his opponents, Cubs past and present, and the circumstances under which the fan saw him. It reminds you not just of Santo and his baseball connections; it reminds you of you.

A bargain, then, at $15, which is what Mad Dog charges for a 1962 Santo. At least, a bargain if you're a Cub fan. I was brought up on the Cardinals.

Mad Dog looked around at the customers on the floor and said, "Most of these guys are 'investors.' They follow the trends up and down in the price guides. If Snoopy magnets were worth anything they'd be running around after Snoopy magnets. But some of them are real fans. Grown-up kids. These were their heroes," he said, waving a hand over his inventory. "They think of Banks and Mays and Mantle as—titans, y'know? So they're here remembering."

He introduced himself and asked if we were looking for anything in particular.

I was going to mention the Schulte card, but just then I got sidetracked. I was flipping through a stack of what they call "commons," or non-star cards, and I saw a 1966 Jose Cardenal.

It gave me a tingle, I'll tell you. I became a kid again instantly. I was back in the exact moment when I'd opened the first pack I ever got.

I grabbed Uncle Rollie's arm.

"Look at that. You *bought* me that card. You bought the pack that card came in."

He looked at it, smiling vaguely.

"I don't recall," he said.

Well, I did. It was right on Front Street in LaPorte, at the grocery. A Friday afternoon, I think; an afternoon, anyway. He bought me *twenty packs*. He said if we were going to St. Louis to see the Cardinals I'd need to know what I was looking at. Slapped a big bill down on the counter. It was the most majestic gesture I'd ever seen. Probably cost him about five dollars. I believe it was on one of those occasions when my dad was on the road. I remember thinking that Uncle Rollie was the one man in town with greatness in him.

I opened them down in his basement tap, sitting in an empty booth. First I stacked the packs on the wooden table . . . four stacks of five packs each. Then

I opened every pack, threw the waxed paper to the side, and stuffed the gum in my mouth. When I was finished I had twenty sticks of gum jammed in my cheek. Then, drooling, I stacked the cards. And the top card when I was finished stacking was Jose Cardenal. Uncle Rollie came over with a dishrag on his shoulder when I was done and said, "You gonna put 'em in teams or alphabetical?"

Jose went on to become a great favorite of mine, and not just because he was my first card. I saw him play for the Cardinals and Cubs in the '70s. He was a wiry, muscular little Cuban who walked as if his feet hurt and held the bat like it was too heavy, but he was fast, and he swung hard, like a slugger. He wore his cap up on top of a giant natural. I liked him because he was a little guy who played as if he was big.

"How much is that card?" I now asked Mad Dog McClure.

He glanced at it.

"Books for three-fifty to seven dollars," he said. "You can have it for three since you're a fan."

I handed over the three dollars and pocketed my remembrance. I would've gladly paid ten.

"Security!"

It was a bellow from our right, from the corner booth next to Mad Dog's. Everyone around us turned to look at a burly, balding, dark-eyed dealer standing under a sign that said LEE VIVYAN COLLECTIBLES. He wore a dark green T-shirt under an unbuttoned Yankee jersey. He was hollering in a deadpan, raspy monotone and staring impassively down the aisle.

"We'll see how long these guys take," he said between calls. "SECURITY! Look at this, he's *walking*."

A bulked-up young man wearing a shirt lettered MERKEL SECURITY strolled up. The dark-eyed dealer waited until he had arrived at the booth and then yelled, "SECURITY!" once more, in his face.

"What can I do for you?" asked the young man, unruffled.

"This kid took a Shaq pin from that guy's booth and put it under his shirt," said the dealer, indicating a wide-eyed twelve-year-old in a Bulls cap and a huge T-shirt, standing in front of him. Why the kid hadn't run away I don't know. He seemed fascinated by the dealer who was turning him in.

"What would you like me to do?" asked Security.

"Oh, you're stumped? I want you to scare him to death, and I want him out of the show," said the dealer. "I thought you guys were supposed to be good. Where's the uniform with the gun?"

"Over by the Wagner."

Merkel Security walked away with the twelve-year-old, and everybody went back to business.

Uncle Rollie was intimidated by the movement and conversation on the floor.

"Everybody's faster than me," he muttered.

"Merkel Security isn't," I said.

Uncle Rollie continued staring at the burly, surly dealer next door. The dealer was now talking with a tall, redheaded man in glasses who had a three-ring notebook filled with cards in nine-pocket plastic sheets. This man looked like he might be a professor, or an impoverished inventor—maybe Mr. Peabody's boy Sherman at thirty-five.

"That's an interesting name . . . Lee Vivyan," the professor was saying, looking at the sign over the booth.

The dealer said nothing.

"What does it sound like? Oh, wait, I get it. Backwards, it's Vivyan Lee." After saying it, the professor giggled involuntarily: "*Ahah*!"

The dealer stood there with his arms folded. You got the feeling he might have heard this twist before. He had a heavy face and the weight of it kind of crushed the levity out of the professor.

"I've got a lot of modern stars," the professor said after an awkward moment, turning his notebook around to give Lee Vivyan a better look. "I've got to let 'em go, though. Getting divorced and I don't wanna . . ." He smiled weakly. "I'll take two hundred. They book for three seventy-five."

Lee Vivyan turned slightly toward us to address his neighbor, Mad Dog.

"It's people like this make the business a joke," he declared flatly. "They think their 1991 cards are valuable antiques."

He reached down to pick up one of his own exhibits in a four-screw Lucite holder, and held it up to the professor.

"This is a 1956 Hank Aaron, showing him—shut

up, wait—sliding in the background, only that isn't him sliding, it's really Willie Mays with a Braves cap painted on. So it's Hank Aaron and Willie Mays on the same card. That's a baseball card, okay?"

He reached for and held up another item.

"Joe DiMaggio's shoelaces, from the spikes he wore when he hit in fifty-six straight. Go ahead, say it: Who's Joe DiMaggio?" He looked at Mad Dog again. "This business is in trouble because it's saturated with people who don't know shit."

Elaborating on this theme, he pointed at one of the poor professor's cards, a Jose Canseco.

"There's more of that card than there are Chinamen. Why would I want it? Why would I want it? Answer me why would I want it. Would I want a handful of sand? And you want two hundred bucks. I'll make a counteroffer: Get the hell away from me."

The professor was offended. "You ought to watch your attitude," he said.

"Yeah, you oughta watch this," responded Lee Vivyan with a casual gesture to his crotch. "Try another table, pal. There are people here as stupid as you, but you gotta shop for 'em. What do *you* want, Pop?"

This last question was addressed to my uncle, who had drifted over to Vivyan as if hypnotized. Now Uncle Rollie blinked, came to the surface, and reached into his overcoat pocket.

"I got this," he said, pulling out Wildfire Schulte.

He got a different reaction than the professor had. Lee Vivyan didn't speak. He froze up looking at the card; his face got completely expressionless. Before my memory got shaky I played poker with a few guys from work, and one of them has a game face like that. When he's holding cards his face could be made out of shale.

I knew we had something when Lee Vivyan did that. A further indication was Mad Dog McClure's neck stretching out of his booth.

Lee Vivyan didn't reach for the card, and he didn't *stare* at it. But he sure noticed it, there in Uncle Rollie's hand.

"Yeah, well . . ." said Lee Vivyan. "That's part of a set, y'know. You'd have to . . . It's not like Frank Schulte was a great player. You'd have to be somebody who was into that set. And I can't tell the condition. It looks . . ."

"It looks pretty goddamn good from here," said Mad Dog McClure.

"Well, it's old," said Uncle Rollie. I didn't know if he was serious or playing the yokel.

"If the condition is all right I might go . . ." Vivyan shrugged. "Four thousand."

A slow, dazed smile spread over Uncle Rollie's face.

"Mister, you got yourself—"

"Thanks," I broke in, to Vivyan. "But we're kind of shopping it around, y'know. We'll get back to you."

He looked at me in a heavy-lidded, who-the-hell-are-you kind of way.

"Only an idiot would pay more than four thousand for that," he said.

"Well, there ought to *be* an idiot in a place this big," I said.

Vivyan shrugged, and seemed to stop himself at the last second from spitting on my shoes. Another new friend lost.

"I'd like to take a look at it," said Mad Dog McClure.

Uncle Rollie was bringing it over to him when all at once there was a popping sound and people began shouting from one corner of the hall, and two big guys with ski masks on blew through a knot of people and came tearing down the aisle past us, scattering everyone in their way. They were young, or they couldn't have gone as fast as they did. And they were big, and they were armed.

I heard somebody yell, "Did they get it? Have they got it?"

I looked around for my people. Charlotte and Uncle Rollie were beside me, but I couldn't find Dillon right away. Then I spotted him down a couple of tables, looking at cards.

By this time I'd noticed something about Dillon . . . that he was a trance kid. You could be talking to him, and something you'd say would trigger a tangential thought, and his eyes would glaze over, he'd be gone. You'd have to give him a shove or call him to bring him back. If he got interested in some task or immediate object, he immersed himself in it; he submerged, and you could . . . well, you could shoot a gun off and he wouldn't notice. He'd done it with X-Men and Wolverine comic books on the way up from Missouri in the car. And he'd done it with a couple of the cartoon books in my apartment. When we first came onto the card show floor, his eyes had widened and his head had begun swiveling. Then he'd found the display he wanted and homed in on it. It was two tables down on the other side of the aisle from us; it featured modern-day cards.

He hadn't reacted to the gunshot from over by the Honus Wagner display, and he hadn't noticed the people hollering. He would have kept staring at the cards and missed the entire incident if one of the runners hadn't brushed him going by. Then he turned around, waking up slowly.

Lee Vivyan had ducked under his display table when the two men ran past. I thought at first he was showing prudence. Then he came up with a gun of his own, vaulted the table, and landed beside us in a crouch, aiming two-handed at their backs as they sprinted down the aisle.

So Dillon, having been distracted from his examination of the inventory two tables down, turned from it to look into the barrel of Lee Vivyan's pistol. It happened so fast that all I could say was, "Hey!"

I'll give the man this: He didn't shoot. He hesitated for a second, while he and Dillon stared bug-eyed at each other.

Charlotte and I bolted over to push Dillon out of the line of fire. Lee Vivyan rose up on tiptoe and danced around trying to get a clear shot off, over or between us.

The two guys in the ski masks skidded around a corner on the cement floor like silent comedians and were gone.

Lee Vivyan came down from his tiptoes. He was furious.

"Fuckin' KIDS all over the place," he said.

Charlotte, her arms around Dillon, was speechless, but she was about the only one. Everybody else was jabbering away and coming out from under the tables. People were streaming back toward the Honus Wagner card exhibit and Merkel Security men were appearing here and there.

A chunky woman in a Cubs cap came up to Mad Dog McClure and said, "They didn't get it. The guard pulled his gun and they ran before they got it."

Uncle Rollie watched as a pair of uniformed cops trotted down the far aisle, weapons drawn.

"Seems like a rough hobby," he said.

CHAPTER TEN

Charlotte searched Dillon's face for signs of emotional trauma, but it may not show up for years. For the time being, the boy seemed exhilarated.

"Wow," he said. He goggled avidly at Lee Vivyan as the dealer put his pistol back under his table.

Charlotte wanted an excuse-me from Vivyan for pointing a gun at her boy, but he was busy reorganizing his inventory, which had gotten disarranged when he jumped over it.

"You almost shot my son," she reminded him.

He glanced up, over at Dillon and back to her. Then he reached over to his discount bin and flipped her a 1983 George Brett with rounded corners.

While Charlotte was gulping for air, Mad Dog McClure offered to buy us all a burger and fries. Dillon admitted he was hungry.

The woman in the Cubs cap turned out to be Mad Dog's wife, Diane. She remained in their booth while he took Uncle Rollie, Charlotte, Dillon, and me off the floor and out the door and down the hallway to a cafeteria.

"Wanted to talk to you about your card," he said.

Dillon was chatty on the way, organizing his hair-raising experience into speech and trying it out on himself and us.

"I turn around and the gun's right here and I'm all 'Whoa!' "

"What in the hell is wrong with that guy?" Charlotte demanded of Mad Dog as we went through the line with our trays. "He almost shot Dillon just for a substitute."

Mad Dog shrugged. "I've done shows with Lee. He cares about the cards, but people in the flesh are not his specialty."

"Man's an ass," said Charlotte flatly.

"Well, he's . . ." Mad Dog seemed to be searching for mitigation while we found a table.

"He's heard that Vivien Leigh joke about maybe a billion times," he said pensively, sitting down. "That could turn a guy sour. Or maybe he was just born mean. I know he's pissed right now. He prides himself on knowing more about baseball and collectibles than any of the rest of us. He grew up watching the Yankees when they always won, and he's got this arrogance, like. Those old Yankee fans . . . some of 'em think they're better than everybody else."

"What's he mad about?" I asked.

"Well, he bets baseball, and sometimes they

don't win when he wants 'em to. And he made a stupid mistake a while back. He bought a thousand Brennan Monroe rookie cards thinking they'd go up, and now Brennan's in prison." He glanced at Dillon and mouthed the word "rape" at Charlotte.

"Rookie cards?" Charlotte asked.

"The first card, Mom," said Dillon. "The first card's always the most valuable."

"Plus a lot of his other eighties and nineties cards tanked when the players went on strike. So, now he says he only trusts Hall of Famers. He's very down on the moderns." Mad Dog took a bite of his cheeseburger and looked at Uncle Rollie. "He's trying to rob you on that card."

"How much would *you* say it's worth?" I asked.

Mad Dog scratched his nose.

"That Higuera set was a very limited issue and they didn't print as many Frank Schultes as they did of the other Cubs. It was my understanding that the card had pretty much disappeared, except for one I saw a picture of in a magazine, and that card was a mess. Fair to Good."

"Beg pardon?"

"Well, cards have grades, with grades between the grades, and that partly determines the price. Mint, Near-Mint, Excellent Plus, Excellent, Very Good-Excellent, Very Good, Good-Very Good, Good, Fair-Good, Fair, Poor. There's some others, but that's it basically. Now, Very Good, for instance, isn't considered very good. That's corner wear, maybe a couple light creases on the card. You won't even get half the

Mint price for Very Good. And Good isn't good. Good is chewed up some. Fair and Poor are cards you put in your bicycle spokes. Collectors are really only interested in cards that are Very Good-Excellent and up. Very little wear. And when they can get Near-Mint in a card from before 1968, they'll pay full price. Near-Mint is just about perfect. Can I see your card again?"

Uncle Rollie took it out and put it on the table in front of Mad Dog, who looked at it over his crossed forearms, not touching it.

"Well, it looks damn good."

"Is 'damn good' good?" I asked.

"Excellent Plus to Near-Mint, I would say. There's professional grading services who might get pickier about it, but you got a nice clean card there. Borders are centered . . . it's still got some shine . . . corners are perfect except for that tiny ding on the lower right. That's the only flaw."

"So it's valuable," said Charlotte.

"Well, there has to be demand. None of this stuff is valuable if nobody cares. In the case of Wildfire Schulte, there's *narrow* demand, but intense, I would say. Certain Cub fans. That set is the last world championship lineup the Cubs ever had. Some Cub fans care about stuff like that."

"Are you a Cub fan?" Uncle Rollie asked.

Mad Dog was silent for a moment, looking down at the table. "Yeah," he said finally.

You could tell he wasn't one of the happy-go-lucky ones.

"Must be tough," said Uncle Rollie.

"I don't talk about it, really, except with people I've known a long time."

Charlotte said, "Well, but what if the Cubs get in the World Series and win? Wouldn't that reduce the value of the card?"

Mad Dog winced. After a moment he said, "Right," in a constricted way.

"I think what Mad Dog is saying is . . . that's not likely," I murmured gently.

We were silent for a moment. Dillon had eaten his burger and was now finishing mine. Mad Dog pulled himself together and looked at Uncle Rollie.

"I think your card's auctionable," he said. "You shouldn't walk around the show floor waving it. I'd recommend contacting a Sotheby's or some other reputable house and letting them put it up."

Uncle Rollie squinted at him. "Who?"

"Auctioneers," I explained.

"What, auction it today?"

"No, it wouldn't be for a while," said Mad Dog. "You have to—"

Uncle Rollie shook his head.

"Nope," he said. "I want to do it today and go home. I got other fish."

Mad Dog looked at him quizzically for a moment, then at me.

"It's his?" he asked.

"It's his."

"Well, maybe I could arrange something for today. I know a few people in town who might be interested. You really want a collector here instead of a dealer. How long you gonna be here?"

"We've got some things to do. We can come back in the afternoon."

"Okay. We're open till ten tonight. They're gonna show the game on the TVs in the hall."

Dillon finished my fries and we got up.

"This is good of you," I said to Mad Dog, who shrugged.

"I saw you were a fan, the way you acted about that Cardenal card," he said. "If you were one of these 'investors' I wouldn't give a shit." He leaned a little closer to mutter, "And I didn't want to see Lee rob an old man, you know. It's bad for the business."

He asked to see the card one last time, in the wide corridor between the cafeteria and Hall C. Uncle Rollie took it out and showed it to him, and Mad Dog gave it a long look. He looked more sad than mad.

"This man played on the last Cub winner," he said. "He looks like he lived a million years ago. Look at that beanie."

Mad Dog brought a sigh up from the floor.

A lot of people say they're "diehard" Cub fans. It seemed to me that Mad Dog McClure was of the type who dies again and again.

"Tell you one thing," he said. "To the right guy this is worth a lot more than what Lee said. Don't bend it. Keep it intact. Keep it clean. Keep it quiet."

On an overhead TV they had a local news show with a couple of guys acting like experts about the night's Cub game. Charlotte called Mad Dog's attention to it, but he shook his head almost fiercely; he wouldn't look at it.

"I can't watch any of that stuff," he said. "I can't stand it. I can watch the game, but I can't listen to the other stuff anymore ... the little jokes ... I can't."

He walked back onto the card show floor.

We came out of the convention center into a pretty day downtown—sunny, clear, with a breeze. A high-masted sailboat was coming up the river and the bridges were going up and down. Charlotte wanted to take some pictures in front of the Michigan Avenue bridge before we split up on our errands, so we went over there.

Mad Dog's remarks about the Schulte had impressed Charlotte. She commemorated the occasion by taking a Polaroid of Uncle Rollie and me holding up the card, and then a close-up of the card by itself. Then Uncle Rollie took one of Charlotte, Dillon, and me. Charlotte gave me the ones of Uncle Rollie and the card for souvenirs.

Looking at the pictures and counting the sunny smiles, I had that impending implosion feeling in my head again. I'd gotten it shortly after Mad Dog Mc-Clure made that remark about a lot more than $4,000.

I can walk down the avenue with the usual bric-a-brac in my pockets and be lighhearted. But if I'm carrying a lot of cash, I get furtive and worry. I glance behind me; I twirl and rotate. Now we had something worth more than any amount of cash I'd ever carried. Even though Uncle Rollie was the one holding the card, I was the one with the responsibility. I mistrusted everyone walking past.

I have this belief, with no statistics to back me up, that you don't generally get robbed if you don't look worth it. I was pleased to see that we didn't appear affluent. In my long overcoat, Uncle Rollie offered no promise of riches. He looked makeshift and poorly assembled. Charlotte's apparel was nice but not gaudy. Dillon and I were in nondescript jeans and jackets—all to the good. I didn't like that we were taking pictures, because that marked us as out-of-towners. Fortunately, Michigan-and-the-river in the middle of a Friday is not a threatening area; it's busy but benign.

The talk about our card's value hadn't fazed Uncle Rollie, because he hadn't retained it.

"Ain't much of a river, is it?" he asked as we stood looking down at it.

"Aren't you nervous or excited?" I asked.

"'Bout what?"

"I know what you should do with that money," said Charlotte eagerly. "Use it to give Rollie something constructive to do. You know Thorpe's boathouse?"

"There is no Thorpe's boathouse."

"That's true, but what if you reopened it?"

I blinked at her. She didn't seem to be making any sense. Charlotte usually makes sense.

"You slowed down," she told Uncle Rollie, "when you sold the tap. You need social activity to get you back up to prime. And I'll tell you, the town needs it, too. Rebuild that boathouse and river people'd be stopping by again instead of *going* by."

She elaborated on this theme, saying that Uncle Rollie could serve as a host and resident raconteur while someone else she didn't name did the routine day-to-day management.

Her idea just delighted Uncle Rollie. He was completely won over when Charlotte suggested that the rebuilt boathouse be named Rollie's Junior.

To me, the idea was peculiar. I took the camera and told Uncle Rollie to stand with Dillon by the bridge. As I took their picture I said to Charlotte, "He overcooks his own dinner up to eight hours. How long do you think that boathouse would be standing if he got it up again?"

Charlotte said, "He's not so bad."

We looked at him. He was playing "Which Hand Is It In?" with Dillon, holding the Wildfire Schulte card behind him, near the bridge railing.

"Let's *see* how bad he is," I said.

Uncle Rollie and I sat beside each other. I wrote my name on a piece of paper. He wrote his name on another piece of paper.

"Now fold them up and put them under your chairs," said Dr. Frye.

Dr. Frye inspires confidence. At least she inspires mine. She's thin, small, and dark, with big black eyes;

her hair and her smock kind of hang on her. She's unfailingly polite and so obviously dedicated that I always feel shiftless by comparison. But then I want my doctor to be a harder worker than me. I've been going to her ever since I moved to Chicago. I recommend her without reservation.

Today, however, she got me a little upset. I'd sort of sprung Uncle Rollie on her when I arrived for my regular appointment, and she didn't have the time to give him a full examination, so she examined him at the same time as me, in the same *way* as me.

He hadn't understood the point of writing his name down and putting it under his folding chair, but he'd done it. He was very docile with Dr. Frye. She has that effect.

She had him repeat a series of numbers. He had some trouble there. He fizzled out on the sequence.

"I remember what I want to remember," he explained, a little defensively.

Then she asked him to take out any photos he had in his wallet and tell her who they were pictures of.

Uncle Rollie produced a couple of old snapshots and stared at them.

"This is my daddy and my brother Loren," he said. He looked at another. "This is me. And this is . . ." He stopped, staring at it, then looked up at me. "Who is this?"

I looked at it. "It's your girlfriend," I said. "In Quincy."

"What's her name?" asked Dr. Frye.

We sat there like a couple of stumps. I couldn't think of it. I looked at Uncle Rollie.

"Katie?" I guessed.

"You're the one who knows who she is," he said. "You ought to know her name."

Dr. Frye asked me where Uncle Rollie lived. Then she asked him where I lived. He got the Chicago part, but didn't know the address or phone number. She asked who the president was.

"Clinton," I said promptly.

"That question was for your uncle, Cooper," said Dr. Frye.

"Oh."

"Clinton," said Uncle Rollie, shrewdly.

She asked a question about early family history. Uncle Rollie was good on this; better than me. He went into a discourse that touched on the meat market his father John had on Chicago's South Side in the first quarter of the century, and his mother, Marian, my grandmother, after whose death during the Depression John Zerbs left Chicago, taking Rollie and baby Loren to Quincy and eventually across the river to LaPorte.

"We were both sweet on your mother, you know," he said to me. "Belle Tyke was a handsome young woman. But your daddy Loren always had a way about him. I'd be talking to Belle, but she'd be watching him. He'd be doing something electrifying. Hanging by his feet from a tree branch or something of that nature. I used to get so aggravated with him, we'd fight. But he had a way, more than me. When it became apparent that him and Belle were . . . well, I withdrew. It was for the best"—he paused here and lowered his voice—"because it developed later that your mother and I can't tolerate each other."

I couldn't compete with him on this material because he lived through it and I'd only maybe heard it a time or two. Some of it was completely new to me . . . I think.

As we sat there, beside each other, it occurred to me suddenly that he was doing better than me. With his detailed reminiscence, he'd forged ahead; he'd answered more questions than I had. I had a light-headed feeling of swirling downward. The presentiment darted into my head that when we were all done, Dr. Frye was going to put me in Uncle Rollie's care.

I wanted more questions. I wanted a chance to come back and beat him.

"Ask us something else," I insisted. "Ask something about current events. Hey, ask him what he ate for breakfast."

Instead, she asked us what those pieces of paper were under our chairs.

We each looked underneath us. I panicked. I looked at Uncle Rollie and I could see he was completely baffled.

I thought, This is what the Zerbses have come to.

I stared at the paper, which I'd stupidly folded in quarters. Had I folded it in half I might've been able to read something. My face was burning. I knew what this meant.

Mark Bailey was the dumbest schoolboy I knew back in LaPorte. Contrary to popular lore, slow kids are not always notable for their sweetness of nature; Mark was also the meanest boy I knew back in LaPorte. He regularly insulted me and my family, and I insulted him back. We fought two or three times a year until high school, which he declined to attend. I had always dismissed his comments about the Zerbses because I considered him only marginally more perceptive than a sockful of sand. But I now had to face the likelihood that I had fallen below even his standard. Wherever Mark Bailey was now, I was willing to bet he could write his name on a piece of paper and remember it two minutes later.

His name.

"My name!" I shouted, leaping from my seat, punching the air.

I won.

After we got our blood pressures taken, I took Dr. Frye aside and asked her how Uncle Rollie was.

"Physically he may be all right. But he shouldn't live alone. Does he?"

"Well, yes, but we're working on that."

"You're going to have to arrange for care."

I nodded. "How about me? How did I do? Not too well. I was better than him, but not by much, huh."

"It wasn't a contest, Cooper."

"Yeah, I know, but I didn't do too well."

"You did quite well," she said with a trace of impatience. "You may feel that you're at a plateau right now, but there's been perceptible improvement and there will be more. Eventually you'll be fine, except that you'll probably always have gaps in the time period just subsequent to the injury."

I nodded again.

"Am I up to Below Average yet?"

The whole episode confirmed my opinion of myself. I didn't have much to say as we left Dr. Frye's office and walked down Kenmore toward the El station.

It was warmer now, and still sunny. Uncle Rollie was alert and chipper. He was captivated by Dr. Frye's neighborhood, which was north and west of the downtown area and which seemed to change radically about every two blocks. We passed from brownstone residential to grungy commercial to vacant lots and a huge brick school. He was particularly intrigued by the graffiti on the walls. I think it appealed to his fishy sense of the obscure. He asked me what all the symbols and words meant. The only one I understood was a big one that said "In$ane Gang$ter$ Will Kill."

We ambled slowly in the nice weather, a couple of Missouri chipkickers.

"Why don't you go on after Charlotte?" he inquired. "What's the matter with you? You oughtn't to be sleepin' with me."

"You may not recall, but I didn't exactly shine on that little intelligence test back there."

"So what?"

"I'm not smart enough for her."

Uncle Rollie snorted.

"If I'd stayed away from women I wasn't smart enough for I wouldn't have any memories at all," he said.

Coming toward us as we walked were half a dozen teenagers in baggy clothes with their caps on backwards. They registered on my eyeballs but not on my brain; ordinarily I'd have crossed to the other side of the street, but I was thinking of Uncle Rollie's remark, and it was daylight, after all. So we strolled right up to each other and all met at the entrance to a little alleyway running parallel to the El tracks.

The lead kid showed me the grip of a pistol sticking up out of his waistband and said, "Get in there."

They hustled us into the alleyway. They were doing a lot of talking; most of it was "motherfucker." Street slang changes from year to year but "motherfucker" is a hardy perennial. They were energetic. They didn't walk; they bounced. They were in a hurry.

Here's something I've never warmed up to about the city: You're so much more likely to get attacked by someone you don't know. In a town like LaPorte, almost all the violence comes from relatives and acquaintances. When Ron Shaw was killed in LaPorte years ago, everybody knew the Jeffries boy did it. It all made sense, even to Ron Shaw. Country life has its ugly side, but at least it's personal. The city is dotted with anonymous land mines. You stroll along okay for a long time, and then step on the wrong patch of ground and somebody blows up in your face.

Of course, the most upsetting aspect of this incident was that we were carrying Uncle Rollie's future. In all my previous ten years in Chicago I'd only been held up once, and that time by a guy in Hyde Park who at least let me hold out carfare. He had said, "I never take a man's last." These kids didn't look so magnanimous.

"Ixnay on the ard-cay," I muttered to Uncle Rollie as they shoved us up against a cement wall.

"What?"

"Shut up," said everybody else in their own way.

"What did you say?" asked Uncle Rollie. "Ixnay what?"

"Forget it. Never mind."

They took our wallets, and my watch. They got my Jose Cardenal card. Then one of them reached into Uncle Rollie's shirt pocket. I held out a hand and stepped forward, saying, "Hey, you got everything that's worth anything."

Two of them grabbed an arm each and held me. The biggest kid, a tall, heavy, fat-faced boy of sixteen or so standing in front of me, told me to shut up again. Then he surprised me by launching himself forward and head-butting me just above my right eye.

It really hurt. His head was like a brick. It didn't knock me out or daze me; nor did it suddenly restore my impaired memory, as a second blow to the head sometimes does in films. It just introduced a blindingly intense pain above my eye. I leaned over and said, "Ohh, God."

Uncle Rollie showed good judgment and restrained his outrage. One of the kids ripped the contents out of his shirt pocket and then they all left. They bounded away, like they were on the moon. We were alone in the alley.

As long as I had thought we might be killed, I'd had something to divert me, but when the kids went away, there was nothing to think about but what we'd lost.

It was clearly my fault. We should have gone and sat in the library until it was time to go back to the show. We shouldn't have been walking around town. Instead of this elaborate fiasco, I'd have saved us time if I'd simply ground the card under my heel when he first showed it to me.

I pulled myself up to my feet. Uncle Rollie was feeling through all his pockets.

"I'm sorry," I said.

"What for?" he asked absently.

"What *for*? For letting those punks get the card."

"Well, yeah, Cooper. You shoulda knocked all their heads together. They only had you by about a thousand pounds and a weapon."

"I shouldn't've brought you to this neighborhood. We aren't gonna get it back, y'know. A mugging is like so what to the cops. They're sorry to hear

about it but that's about it. Those kids'll probably
throw it away, anyhow."

Uncle Rollie shook his head and said, "Nah."

"Nah, what? You think they'll get to feeling
sorry and bring it back?"

"They won't throw it away," he said, looking
serenely in the direction they'd taken, "because they
didn't get it."

"Say again?"

"Didn't get it."

"Whaddya mean? Why not?"

" 'Cause I didn't have it."

I stared at him through my headache. It sounded
like babble, as though he'd finally walked off the pier.
Then I noticed that he wasn't wearing the overcoat
I'd given him when we left my apartment.

"You forgot and left it at the doctor's office," I
said slowly.

He smiled as if to say how elementary the whole
thing was.

"They got to get up pretty early to get that card
from *me*."

Whereupon, to my astonishment, he cackled, offered me an arthritic high five and launched into a
kind of strut-dance right there in the alley, singing
along with himself. I couldn't have been more surprised if he'd whistled for his wonder horse and rid-
den off in a cloud of dust.

He used to sing in the tap, along with the juke-
box or the radio, in a toneless, cheerful way. "Yesterday's Winner Is a Loser Today." "Stagger Lee."

On his own record player, he'd play this old song by Hoagy Carmichael, "Moon Country." And some old records by Louis Jordan. He didn't confine himself to country and western. Anything with a good lyric was what he liked.

Right now he was a sight, cakewalking past a dumpster, croaking out a tune about the coffee in Brazil.

I had to laugh. It was so unexpected. And I was so happy we hadn't lost the card . . . well, it was infectious. I'm going to admit this here: I joined him for a minute. We both took time out for a little dance, there in the alleyway. A few steps. The Zerbses, triumphant.

I stopped dancing when it occurred to me what exactly we were celebrating:

We had out-dumbed 'em. They couldn't steal it because we were too stupid to bring it with us.

Uncle Rollie finally stopped as well, in order to bend over and cough. I patted him on the back for a few moments while he recovered.

"You know," I said to him, "this is not a dependable strategy."

CHAPTER ELEVEN

Another thing about Dr. Frye is if you leave your priceless baseball card in an overcoat in her office, she doesn't go through the pockets. So we had Wildfire again when we went back downtown on the El, using change her receptionist loaned us. We'd reported our mugging to the police, who were sympathetic.

It was about three o'clock, and we weren't due back at the card show to meet Charlotte and Dillon until four. My big idea was to go by my work and get us a bodyguard.

The Neatly Chiseled Features syndicate office is on the eighth floor of the Times Building on Wabash. I knew that I could get some petty cash there. And we'd be safe there. And Big Stan was there.

And I also wanted Uncle Rollie to see where I worked, there in the long building by the Chicago River. I still had some residual pride in the distance I'd come from LaPorte.

I remember the first time I went to work in the building. I was hired to stuff envelopes and run the printers in the production department. As I entered through the revolving doors on my first day, I felt like one of those characters in the theme song of an old sitcom: "Nothing can stop me now." It was glamorous. I felt I was dead center, smack in the hub of the wheel. Quite a change from LaPorte, where if you stand in your yard at night you can easily imagine that you're missing something.

As the years went by, the romance wore off some. The excitement was still there, but it was nervous excitement. Tension. I got promoted.

I caught some mistakes in the columns I was stuffing and I got taken out of production and made an editorial assistant. Later I became an assistant editor, which is slightly more elevated and responsible than editorial assistant. Then I became an associate editor.

I became responsible for the accuracy of political, advice, and cooking columns that we syndicate to newspapers all over the country. I had to make sure there were no mistakes in any of that material. Editors at Neatly Chiseled are taught to worry about everything, and pretty soon I did.

I kept waiting for the day I'd let some error go by that would bring the entire weight of law and public censure down on top of the Times Building, crushing it and me. Or when I'd let a recipe go out that killed thousands. I picked up a lot of information in those columns—I became familiar with the ingredients to several hundred dishes—but there was a cost in peace of mind.

After I hurt my head, I missed some mistakes. No one died as a result, but I was reassigned to comics, where you have more turnaround time. I now pored over each panel laboriously, and had no further expectations of advancement.

When I brought Uncle Rollie in, Big Stan was back in the production department, muscling some huge filing racks. I'm still astounded that I ever walked away from an altercation with him. His arms are in the comic book superhero style.

Billy Garner was back there, too, sweating it out in a corner. Production is pretty much Stan's bailiwick; if he wants to bring a guest back there to dry out, no one's likely to yell at him.

"Took him to a meeting last night," Big Stan said to me. "He stood up."

"Hello, Billy," I said.

Billy nodded and sucked on a Coke can, devoting his attention to the envelope stuffers across the room.

Casey, the president, came back looking for something, brisk and businesslike with his hair combed straight back for less wind resistance, and I introduced Uncle Rollie to him. Casey's eyes widened behind his glasses.

"So this is the gentleman with the baseball card," he said. "Pleased to meet you. How do you like our shop?"

"I'm a great admirer of people who live by the

written word," said Uncle Rollie. "I haven't seen much, we just got here."

"Let me show you around," said Casey, taking his arm. Since this fit in perfectly with my two-part master plan, I gladly sent Uncle Rollie off in Casey's grip. Then I turned back to Big Stan, who stood like a forklift with three boxes of comic originals in his arms.

"Were you serious about making amends?" I asked.

He brightened instantly. I noticed his skin was much clearer and less veiny than it used to be.

"You tell me what I can do," he said simply.

"A little moonlighting. I need a bodyguard for a baseball card. Starting right after work."

He agreed enthusiastically on the condition that he not be paid. He had changed more than a movie of the week would have allowed him to.

"How's Irene?" I asked him.

His expression became grave, embarrassed, and sympathetic.

"She wants you to know she appreciates all you did. She really likes you as a friend, Cooper."

"Well, you know," I said.

"You can hit me if you want to."

"I'd rather not, Stan, I'd probably just hurt myself again. I'm glad you're back together, really."

Big Stan's eyes filled with tears. It alarmed me. He shook his head to reassure me.

"You get emotional in your first year," he explained.

We agreed to meet at the card show just after five o'clock, and I went off to the art department.

Dee Francona is a short, stocky guy with a little potbelly and big beautiful teeth. He is the art department at Neatly Chiseled. We have about forty strips in the stable, and he is their valet. He draws the mustache on Big Herbie when the cartoonist forgets to put it there. He fixes the lettering errors. He shoots the strips with the stat camera and gets them ready in weekly batches to be printed and sent to the newspapers that buy them. In his spare time he works on his own strips, which he hasn't been able to sell yet. He can work in most any style, but he can't write as well as he draws. If he could, he'd be in five hundred papers.

He was eating a bagel with cream cheese when I came into his cubicle.

"What are *you* doing here?" he wanted to know.

I took out Charlotte's Polaroid of the Schulte card and put it on one of his drawing boards.

"Can you duplicate that?" I asked.

He leaned forward to look at it. "What is it?"

"It's a 1909 cigar box baseball card."

"Cardboard?"

"Yeah."

Dee examined it, chewing. Then he sat back.

"No," he said. "I can't duplicate a card from that. I could do an approximation, but it wouldn't fool anybody."

"My uncle's not just anybody."

The scheme had come to me after we got

mugged. If I had a copy of the Schulte card, I could switch it with Uncle Rollie's and personally protect the real one. I didn't think it would have to be very good to fool him until the auction. It would go in a plastic sleeve anyhow, so it wouldn't have to feel the same.

I was trying to be responsible. I don't have any kids, and I don't support any overseas. Uncle Rollie is my only child. And although this switch would be dishonest, I thought it justified. The mere fact that I could think of it indicated to me that I was still slightly sharper than he was.

Dee had a light day and was willing to help me out as soon as he finished his bagel. In payment, I agreed to give him a Joe Martin "Porterfield" original he'd admired on my office wall from time to time.

Then it was off to find Uncle Rollie. He wasn't in word processing or the conference room, so I went to Casey's office. I heard Casey talking as I walked past his secretary's desk and approached his open door: "So it's a deal, then."

On hearing these words I was struck with a nameless fear. No, that's wrong; it wasn't nameless.

Casey moved up along with me in the company, only faster and farther. He came up out of the sales department like a missile. He still goes on the road occasionally, even though he's president now. He can sell comic strips to editors who don't want them, who have no space for them. He can convince them to cancel strips they already have and like, to make room for one they don't particularly want. He can do this, he told me once when we were drinking, because he uses what actors call "the magic if." He believes everything he says at the time he says it. "I convince myself," he said. "And I project that conviction."

Casey tells you exactly what he thinks, with this codicil: he thinks it *now*, with no guarantees about a minute from now. He embraces many faiths. I can't really tell you what long-standing beliefs he has. He's remained loyal to the Cubs and his own career, but beyond that I wouldn't care to go.

Back when Casey was still a salesman, we introduced a strip called Crumbunny which was so bad it made people angry to look at it. We only went ahead with it because the president was a friend of the artist. Casey hated it on sight. But when he hit the road with it, he told editors that Crumbunny had a delayed effect. That it stayed in the mind and made you laugh days or even weeks later. He'd begin laughing then, pointing to a sample strip the editor was staring at. "This one just hit me," he'd say. "I meant it, too," he told me later. "I got to where that shit cracked me up."

He sold Crumbunny to several papers, but the delayed effect never kicked in and the feature was canceled everywhere inside of a year. None of the editors doubted Casey's sincerity, though. You couldn't. He was that good.

Now, hearing him say, "It's a deal, then," I hurtled forward and charged into Casey's office as if I'd been thrown.

Casey was sitting on the front edge of his desk,

holding the Schulte card and beaming down at Uncle Rollie, who was hunched over in a chair, peering at what looked like one of our standard syndicate contracts.

"Casey!"

He transferred his smile from Uncle Rollie to me.

"Cooper," he said, "your uncle's an extraordinary man. This fish poetry of his could be the biggest thing since Calvin and Hobbes."

"He's signin' me up, Cooper!" said Uncle Rollie. "A five-year contract and he's gonna sell the poetry to the newspapers, like I always wanted you to do. *And* he's givin' me two thousand dollars."

I glared at Casey.

"I notice he's holding the card," I said. "How about *that*?"

"I don't care if he gets the card as long as my fish get in the paper," said Uncle Rollie.

"Your uncle," said Casey, "gets the two thousand *and* the five-year contract."

"All that obligates him to do," I told Uncle Rollie, pointing at Casey, "is give you fifty percent of whatever they make on your feature. If they make nothing, you get fifty percent of that."

Uncle Rollie looked blankly at me.

"Don't you see? They take a sample of your fish writing to a newspaper editor, and say, 'You want this?' The guy says, 'Not with a gun to my head.' The end. Contract obligation fulfilled. You sit by the window with a shawl on your lap and he gets the card from you for two thousand dollars."

Casey wasn't smiling anymore.

"Excuse us," he said to Uncle Rollie. Then he led me over to his big river-view window and glared at me.

"I want you to take a minute to think over what you're saying," he said.

"Oh, yeah? Listen, Casey. People say my uncle's got diminished capacity. Well, I've been with him a few days and lemme tell you: they ain't lyin'. But it's not him that's got the problem here, it's *you*, taking advantage of him like that."

Casey's glasses were flashing.

"You're calling me a liar."

"If you want to condense it."

He was full height now, five nine, beginning to vibrate and hiss.

"This," he said clearly, "is the thanks I get."

"Thanks for what? An office tour?"

"For *carrying* you for six months when you couldn't earn half your paycheck. When you couldn't read anything tougher than Uncle Chunky. I could've let you go, Cooper. People *said* I should let you go."

That was a direct hit. It hurts when people say you're incompetent in front of family.

"I kept you on," Casey continued, "because I thought you deserved a chance to recover." He was a quivering tower of virtue in suspenders. "Six months I've carried you."

"Okay," I said quietly, with as much dignity as I could find lying around. "All right. Maybe so. So you're entitled to cheat my uncle, is that the idea?"

"I've made him a legitimate offer."

"Bullshit."

I can't believe I said that during office hours, sober. It's indicative of how mad I was that I went on from there.

I noticed his Billy Williams bat in the corner by the bookcase.

"Cub fan, my ass," I said. "You're no Cub fan. Cub fans don't tell a guy they're going to syndicate his fish poetry when they know it won't sell. I don't care how much 'magic if' you hand him and yourself, you can't sell that stuff and you know it."

That pretty much exhausted my opinion, so I looked out the window at the river.

"I'm sorry you see it that way," Casey said stiffly. "But isn't it up to him?"

Uncle Rollie had been watching us with his mouth open. Now he maneuvered his way out of his chair and up to Casey.

"Can you get my fish in the papers or not?" he demanded.

Casey pushed his glasses up on the bridge of his nose and looked at us, exasperated. He opened his mouth and closed it.

Then he handed the card back to him.

Uncle Rollie sighed deeply.

"I'm disappointed in you," he said to Casey. "A man in your position is supposed to have vision."

He walked past me and out the door, telling me to come on.

Casey and I glanced at each other and then

around at the window and the bookcase.

"Well," I said, "I've called you a cheat and you've called me dead weight. That oughta do it."

Casey looked at me sadly.

"What's it been, eight years?" he said.

Then he called Security and gave me half an hour to get my personal effects and my uncle out of the building.

"Policy," he explained.

I woke up outside, walking down Wabash with a cardboard box full of old proofs and signed originals. My predecessor as comics editor, when he was fired, inadvertently left behind an old Pogo book autographed by Walt Kelly, so I had that, too, on top of the stack. I had a paycheck, because it was Friday. That was the complete bright side.

In the years since arriving in Chicago, my ambition had eroded. From unformed plans of becoming famous for some reason, I had drifted into a kind of day-to-day getting along that I only questioned on my birthday.

But it's one thing to lose your momentum, and another to lose your job.

I'd lost my *job*.

I felt shrunken and exposed, vulnerable to everything. It wasn't far from where I was to where my father ended up. I could get there from here—with a stopover on the street. There was $1300 in the bank, not counting the last paycheck. When that was gone it would be winter. Walking along, I noticed how lit-

tle earth there was to fall on in the Loop. It's all metal
and stone—sidewalk, buildings, avenue and El pillars.
Flesh and bone leaves no impression on these sur-
faces, I thought with maudlin satisfaction. Only
blood. You lie there, squashed by the city. They cart
you away, and your blood soaks into the pavement.
The pigeons peck at it.

As we trudged on toward the convention hall, I
couldn't help comparing my state of mind with that
of my uncle, whose cheery demeanor was becoming
a strain. I was finding him considerably more trying
than when I saw him once a year.

He still held the card. That was all right. But he
persisted in revealing it to total strangers, including
the shill outside a Kinzie Street exotic dance club featuring "Misty Rue and Her Twin Bazookas."

"Ya comin' in or not?" this guy asked us, ignoring the card.

Uncle Rollie looked from the posters of Misty to
me, expectantly.

"We're low on cash," I said to the shill.

"Major credit card. First show in ten minutes."

"Thanks. Not in the mood."

I used my box of office belongings to push Uncle
Rollie on down the street.

"Hey, she'll *get* ya in the mood," I heard from
behind me.

CHAPTER TWELVE

By the time we got to the card show, I had cranked up my self-pity to the point where I was thoroughly put out with Uncle Rollie.

The way I saw it, if I hadn't brought him to work with me I'd still have my job—never mind that my boss didn't think I deserved it. And if I hadn't taken him with me to the doctor's office, I'd still have my wallet and watch. Now I had nothing.

And he still wouldn't let me hold the card.

Attendance had increased slightly at the show. The Cub-Dodger playoff game was due to start pretty soon. There were three overhead TVs in Hall C itself and another in the hallway outside.

Passing Lee Vivyan's booth on the way to see Mad Dog McClure, Uncle Rollie and I stopped to listen to a discussion Vivyan was having with a muscular little guy with a ponytail.

"You can have the Aaron," Vivyan was saying,

"and the '55 Koufax. Not the shoelaces."

The short man said something I couldn't hear.

"Is that what Ronnie says?" said Vivyan. "Well, here's what I say: he'll get the rest. He can wait till Monday. He's not hurting."

The little guy said something else, and Lee Vivyan blew up.

"Hey, Carl, you and Fat Ronnie Buoniconti and every hump in his stable can fuck a rolling doughnut. You don't tell me whether these laces are authentic. You don't tell me about the Barry Halper collection. Barry Halper doesn't have everything DiMaggio ever wore. *Jes*us, I'm tired of people who don't know what they're talking about. Here's Homer and Jethroe," he went on, noticing Uncle Rollie and me. "Tooth fairy leaves 'em an old card and they want to get rich like fuckin' Jed Clampett."

He leaned toward the short man and spoke to him flatly and heavily.

"I know what this stuff is worth. I might lose on a ball game but I don't lose on this stuff. And you don't get DiMaggio's shoelaces. Fat Ronnie'll get his money after the playoffs. If he don't like it, he knows where I am. But he don't get the laces. He don't *deserve* the laces. Sox fan. Chicago juice. BFD."

The short man Carl shook his head, wincing. He looked mortified. He said, "Lee, you're embarrassing me here."

There was a pause.

Lee Vivyan flicked a glance at him and sort of shut down. He looked uncomfortable.

"What did I say?" he asked. "Maybe I went overboard, what did I say? I said he'd get his money."

"I don't know, Lee, I'm still back there with the rolling doughnut. I can't go back and repeat that. I can't tell him you said that in front of people."

He gestured at Uncle Rollie and me. Lee Vivyan shot us an even dirtier look than usual, then switched to dignified contrition for Carl.

"Never mind them. They don't count. I got excited there and said a couple things I didn't mean. I apologize for any disrespectful language and I'd appreciate it if you'd forget it." He turned back to us and added, "Maybe you guys should go look at the exit sign, it lights up."

I pulled Uncle Rollie along and we fetched up at Mad Dog McClure's booth to find him looking up apprehensively at pre-game programming on one of the overhead TVs. He nodded when he saw us. Diane McClure offered to let me put my box of belongings under their table, and I took her up on it.

"He's really doing it, he's starting Henley," Mad Dog announced to no one in particular. "I'm not going to say that's suicide. I think it. I don't say it." He rubbed his face with both hands, then slapped it as though with after-shave and focused on me.

"I talked to some people on our mailing list," he said. "There are about half a dozen major collectors in town that I know, but I could only reach two of them. They both said they'd be here after the game, which'll probably be about closing time. They're ready to bid on it if it's in good shape. Have you still got it?"

Uncle Rollie began going through his pockets. I watched him, fuming.

"This card," I observed, "is the only thing that's holding us up, and we can't even remember which pocket it's in."

"We been doin' all right," said Uncle Rollie, finally producing it with a flourish. "I think we make a good team."

"Good team? Did you say good team?"

"Yeah."

"Tweedledum and Tweedle-dumber."

"Hi," said Dillon at my elbow.

I jumped, startled, and saw Charlotte behind him. She was breathless; her eyes were wide and her smile was a dazzler.

"So! What's new?" she asked.

"I can tell something's new with *you*," I said.

"They liked it. It's going up in the flagship Mr. Green Genes restaurant on Ontario. They're hanging it down there now," she said conversationally, nodding as she spoke. Then she screamed a single high note, sustaining it for about five seconds.

She was so happy I caught it from her. I was going to hug her, but she hugged me first. Now we were both breathless.

"It's thanks to you, honey," she told Dillon, hugging him, too. "If I hadn't been so bored watching you when you were little I never would've stuck with it."

"Is there going to be a ceremony?" Uncle Rollie asked. "They gonna pull down a sheet and there it is?"

"God, no." She laughed. "They'll slap it up on the wall and forget about it. But they're going to slap prints up on the walls of all the other franchises, too."

"How many?" I asked.

"I don't know. *They* don't know. Depends on whether anybody likes their genetically spliced squamatoes."

"But it could be like being in the first Colonel Sanders with an option on the rest, right?"

"Some salad chain's gonna make it," Charlotte allowed. "It might be Mr. Green Genes."

"Well, there ya go."

"We're gonna be rich," said Dillon solemnly.

"No, hon," said Charlotte.

"Are we gonna be partly rich?"

"How about you?" she asked me. "How's it going?"

"Oh, well, you know. When the Zerbses team up, things get done."

I told her briefly what we'd accomplished so far. When I got to the part about losing my job, her eyes widened again.

"Well, then, you should do what I said," she told me. "You and Rollie should go in together on Thorpe's boathouse."

"Hey, how about that?" said Uncle Rollie, suddenly all sparkle. "The two of us. Like when you helped me in the summer at the tap."

145

"What is this thing about Thorpe's boathouse?" I asked. "Is there something buried under it?"

Charlotte showed a flicker of annoyance.

"Yeah, Cooper. LaPorte's buried under it."

"That's a little dramatic, isn't it?"

"When that place was open they started the annual swimming race to Oak Bluff from it. All the family boats stopped there and everybody came up to eat. They had dances there. People came from *other* towns to *our* town. Now there's no reason to."

"I don't get where we come in."

"Sure you do. Rollie's got experience. He ran a tap. You used to help him. You could help him again."

Well, she had a point. I had worked for him a couple of summers, and helped him run the concession stands for town ball games and a small traveling circus that came to LaPorte. I'd liked it. I'd felt briefly indispensable. And the town probably could use somebody to revive Thorpe's riverside establishment.

But not us. Not now. We weren't up to it.

"Food ordering," I said. "Withholding forms. Health insurance. *Employees*. Maintenance. How about the next flood?"

"You're not looking at your positives," she insisted.

"Charlotte . . . he and I took a test together at the doctor's office and I don't know which of us charted out to be Beavis. You want to make entrepreneurs out of two guys who need their mittens clipped to their sleeves."

Her expression went from shock to a mix of pity and contempt. Then she looked like she might cry. Then she turned and stormed off. Her anger turned her special amble into more of a sashay.

I felt I hadn't explained my position very well, so I followed her, first telling Dillon to stay with Uncle Rollie until I got back.

Charlotte stopped at the end of a snaky line of people waiting to get Willie McCovey's autograph. As I caught up with her, she was breathing as if she'd been in a sprint.

"Are you all right?" I asked.

"I am bathed in sweat," she said.

"Well . . . you smell fine."

"I am this close"—she held up a finger and thumb, nearly pinched—"to a collapse. All I do is things I'm afraid to do. Coming up here, going to see those Green Genes people . . . even that damn little Billy last night . . ." She shuddered. "He makes me think of spiders. When I was with Lloyd, do you know I had to deal with every mouse and spider that got in the house? He wouldn't approach anything that crawled or skittered. After that movie came out he said he had arachnophobia. I said, 'Lloyd, who doesn't? We can't both just stand here and scream.' "

"You fooled me," I said. "I thought you were the all-new fearless Charlotte."

She shot me a glance.

"You fooled me, too," she said. "I thought you were the old fearless Cooper. This is not," she said to the back of the guy standing in front of her, "the

Cooper Zerbs who carried me home when I broke my leg."

She makes such a big deal of that incident. All I did was, she was on a seesaw glider on the swingset the Dyers had in their backyard. She was just four. I was six and I was there one day, with Stevie Dyer and a couple other kids. She was on one glider seat and went to cross forward to the other, and she tried to pull herself across while the glider was going back and forth. Somehow she got her leg twisted in that tubing that comes down. I was next to her in a regular swing and I didn't see her leg break, but I heard it, and of course her screaming.

It's true that I tried to carry her home. I remember our shadows on the ground, with my cowboy hat on top, as I struggled along with her. But I had to let her down from time to time. I wasn't tall or strong enough to hold her off the ground very long.

"If you recall," I told her now, "I had to drag you most of the way. I caused you more suffering and damage than if I'd left you in the backyard."

"I don't care. Back then you had some balls."

"Not to speak of."

"Sand, then. Guts."

We had moved up in the line. Willie McCovey was sitting twenty feet ahead, wearing a beige cap, signing baseballs and photographs as they were handed to him by men and women our age or older.

"This Thorpe's boathouse thing is not about guts," I told her. "It's about brains. And I've depreciated in that area."

148

She'd been smoldering up to this point, but now she ignited, turning on me.

"I'll tell you what it is. You just won't do anything tough. You left home because it was tough being a Zerbs. You want someone to live with your uncle because he's too much for you. Your job got too tough, and I expect *we'd* be too tough. I hope you've got a nice soft pillow, Cooper."

She turned away to see how close we were to McCovey.

"Hey!" I said, turning her back. "I've been trying not to weigh you *down*. I've been trying to be *noble*. If you think I don't want you back you're dumber than I am. I don't even *notice* other women."

Charlotte gestured for me to tone it down. It had been okay for her to tear into *me* in a crowd, but now that I had the floor she was suddenly conscious of bystanders. I was mad, though, so I went on regardless.

"If I still had the brains I was born with," I said, "you couldn't get rid of me. I even like your *kid*. So don't tell me about tough. I've had time to go over it. Being *without* you was tough. I was curled up in a ball for about a year. I forgot everything else but I didn't forget that."

We had arrived at the signing table. Willie McCovey looked up at me, pen poised.

"Gimme a break," I told him.

"I'm just here to sign," he said. "I'm not trying to get in your way."

"Can you write 'Best wishes, Dillon'?" asked

Charlotte, handing him a baseball. "That's D-I-L-L-O-N."

"All right," he said.

"So you're disqualifying yourself from everything," she said to me, "because you think you're—what? Mentally challenged?"

"A feeb," I said.

"You say that, but you don't look any different to me," she said. "I think it's an excuse. I haven't seen you do anything dumb."

Well, I know a dare when I hear one. She was right there in front of me, looking up into my eyes. First she'd been happy and then she'd been mad, so she'd been radiating warmth of one kind and another for the last ten minutes. She was exercising a powerful magnetic pull; I felt as though if I relaxed I'd run into her.

It occurred to me that I'm not really that noble.

And there was no point worrying about disappointing Charlotte if she was already disappointed.

And it would be refreshing to do the wrong thing on purpose for a change.

"I'll show you dumb," I said.

First kisses don't always work out. Some people's mouths don't match up. Some people's kissing styles don't match either. Sometimes you each turn your head the same way and wind up chasing each other around the block.

But Charlotte and I were old partners. And even though we hadn't tried it in about eleven years, we remembered our technique. In fact, this long gap acted as a buildup, so once we got started, we revved up pretty quickly and began embellishing.

When I felt her coming at me as hard as I was at her, I lost track of where exactly we were. I didn't care how dumb I was. If you feel something strongly enough you lose your self-consciousness.

Of course we were surrounded by people; we were still in the head of the autograph line. The people there had come to see the Hall of Fame first baseman of the San Francisco Giants, not two anonymous people furiously gulping each other. I believe I heard McCovey's voice asking, "Why'nt *you* sign?" I have a vague recollection of some kids making that sardonic rising-wave "wooohhh" sound. I had a rising-wave sound in my ear, anyway. Somebody may have called for Security.

Then I heard a voice from above and behind me, repeating something.

"Where's the old guy?" it said.

"Where's the old guy?" "Where's the old guy?" The question gradually brought me back to my surroundings. It disturbed me. It seemed to echo, like in an old forties film noir ("You're a LOSER-oozer-oozer."). It occurred to me that my last hit on the head, from the kid in the alley, might have introduced audible, nonexistent voices inside my skull, like so many people have.

Charlotte and I disengaged slowly, and I turned. Looking up, I saw Big Stan Cornell smiling at me, amused. Behind him, as if in his pocket, was Billy Garner, staring past me at McCovey.

"Way to go, Cooper. Where's your uncle?" said Big Stan.

I stared at him.

"Oh, shit."

Charlotte scolded Dillon for it, but it wasn't his fault and I told her so; I knew whose fault it was. When we got back to Mad Dog's booth, Dillon was across the aisle, dickering solemnly with another dealer over the price of his "grab bag" envelopes. The boy looked around blankly when we asked him where Uncle Rollie was.

Mad Dog and Diane McClure hadn't seen him leave; he'd been there one minute, gone the next.

"Lost the old man, huh?" said Lee Vivyan from next door. "That's too bad."

I ran to the men's room. He wasn't there. He wasn't in any of the nearby aisles. I ran out to the hallway and had him paged. I came back to Mad Dog's booth. Charlotte, Dillon, Big Stan, and Billy Garner returned from aisle reconnaissance. No one had seen him. He didn't respond to the page.

The inside of my head felt like it was crumpling. This wasn't just forgetting my name on a piece of paper. This was negligence. This was letting down the family.

"Would he leave?" asked Big Stan.

"Maybe he decided to go back to LaPorte," said Charlotte.

"Maybe he thought he could get into the ball game," said Diane McClure, indicating the overhead

TV Mad Dog was watching.

I couldn't stand around. I had to run again. I told Big Stan and Charlotte to make sure he wasn't in the building, and I took off, out of Hall C.

I ran down the big corridor and out the revolving door Uncle Rollie and I had entered by. Outside, it was downtown; it was rush hour; it was Friday. People were spilling out of all the buildings.

I felt hot, as Charlotte said she had when she couldn't find Dillon that time. My bloodstream was rushing panic and guilt to every extremity. Uncle Rollie was the only person I'd ever been responsible for, and I had lost him.

People gave me plenty of room as I stood on the street corner, calling his name frantically and uselessly. I must have sounded dangerously lost myself; a grown boy calling for his Uncle Rollie.

I knew he could be anywhere: wandering in an office building, fallen in the river, rolled already and thrown off the Wabash El platform onto the concrete. Or, almost certainly, none of those places but some other place I'd never think of. He could be calling for me.

Now and then I read in the paper about these poor parents whose children disappear.

If I ever have a child, I swear I'll keep him on a leash. I'll paste him in my hat.

CHAPTER THIRTEEN

After tearing around the convention center I ran out of wind and had to alternate walking and trotting, back toward Neatly Chiseled Features. I didn't have much of an idea. I thought maybe he'd gone to revive the subject of syndicating his fish poetry with Casey. After Neatly Chiseled I'd try my apartment. After that, the police.

The same shill was standing outside the Club Wow—the strip palace featuring Misty Rue and Her Twin Bazookas—as I came up to it. He smirked at me, and I slowed up.

"There ya are," he said.

"Say, listen, did the old guy I was with before go by here?"

The guy kept smiling.

"He didn't go by."

I stared at him. I squinted at the posters on the wall.

"Is he in there?"

"Ya got me, Slick. I just took a break."

I sighed, and cocked my head to look at the guy. I couldn't figure out if he was saying yes or no, so I walked past him and inside.

The Club Wow seemed cramped, but it might have been spacious; it was very dark after the street. There wasn't much light except for the small stage and runway.

Misty Rue, the headliner, was up there, moving to an old song, "Whip Appeal," by Babyface. I recognized her from her photos outside.

Now when I told Charlotte that I didn't notice other women, I meant it in essence, but I exaggerated to make a point. Some women are impossible not to notice and Misty Rue fell into this category. Even desperate and distracted as I was, I couldn't pretend she wasn't there. She went beyond statuesque; she was, I would say, monumentally curvaceous. According to one of the posters outside, Misty was "100 percent natural." If so, she represented nature at its most extreme. The billowing and sloping from bust in to waist and back out to hips was so radical it made your eyeballs hurt to keep up with it.

And yet somehow she carried it all well. Practice, I guess. A pleasant smile and nice legs, too. Maybe a half pound too much eye shadow. A graceful if not brilliant dancer. All in all, a stupefying sight if you were just in off the street.

There were tables all over the floor, three on each side of the runway. Five of these were occupied, and as my eyes adjusted I saw that Misty was aiming her augmented measurements at one table in particular. Seated there was my uncle, looking astounded, with a girl on his lap.

I walked over to their table and sat down in a chair just behind them. I watched Uncle Rollie watching the show for a moment, and I waved hello to the pretty Asian girl who was wriggling on his lap. Misty leaned forward to give Uncle Rollie a heavy-lidded pout and a shake. When she straightened up and moved on down the runway, I leaned forward myself and observed,

"No people like show people."

He jumped a little and turned to see me.

"Oh, hi, Cooper."

"I couldn't find you there for a while. What is it that you think you're doing?"

"Well," he said, shifting in his seat under the girl, "I been having trouble remembering things, so I thought I'd take in something so amazing that I couldn't forget it."

The song faded out and Misty, having executed a pivot that nearly wiped out the tables on the far side of the runway, left the stage.

"She likes me," said Uncle Rollie.

"We all like you," said his lap partner.

A few moments later Misty reappeared on the floor in a sequined halter and a kind of transparent shawl, and sat down next to him.

"How'd I do, Uncle Rollie?" she asked.

While I was digesting that, a bullet-headed waiter

appeared with three bottles of "champagne" on a tray. He put the bottles down and Uncle Rollie, to my horror, pulled a hundred-dollar bill out of his shirt pocket and handed it to him.

"Who's your friend?" Misty asked her new uncle.

"I'm his nephew," I said, standing up. "He's *my* uncle Rollie."

Misty remained calm. "He said he was mine, too. He says I remind him of somebody."

"That seems unlikely," I said, looking her up and down. Then I turned to him and said, "C'mon."

"*Why?*" he asked. Not unreasonably, from his point of view. Sitting in a dark bar, reminiscent of his old one, with one babe on his lap and a Marvel super-babe seated next to him, he had little to look forward to outside.

"I want to talk about finances," I told him. "Your nieces will still be here when you get back. Would you let him up, please?"

The other girl, whose name I heard as Sheena, sulked a little bit, but got off his lap. I helped Uncle Rollie up and held him by the arm while I propelled him past the waiter and out the door to the sidewalk. We moved a few yards away from the entrance and I turned him around to face me.

"Goddamn it, Mom was right about you. You don't have that much sense. You know what you've done here? Where's the card?"

He felt in his pockets and looked stricken.

"It's gone, isn't it. You sold it. You got any

money left, or did you put it all between Misty's bazookas?"

I was beside myself. I flapped around in a circle
on the sidewalk; I couldn't help it.

"I don't believe it. We've been here *one day*. And
we've lost everything. Our wallets, my watch, my job,
your card . . . We're *bums* now. Do you understand?
Can you see it coming at you through the fog? You
are going into a *facility*, and I ought to be in one with
you. . . . Misty *Rue*? What in the hell were you thinking of? Infancy?"

I was arrested in my tirade by the sight of Uncle
Rollie, standing in a collapsed kind of way there on
the sidewalk, his eyes pooling up.

"I didn't want to sell it," he said brokenly. "Fella
took it."

I felt like some district attorney who had just finished a ringing closing statement, flaying the defen-
dant up one side and down the other, only to
remember suddenly that I'd done the murder myself.
I was that ashamed and remorseful when Uncle Rollie
told me, "Fella took it."

I stepped forward and pulled his head to my
shoulder so I wouldn't have to look at his face.

"I'm sorry," I said. "I'm sorry. I left you alone,
it was my fault."

"I didn't want to sell it. I knew it wasn't right.
Fella *made* me."

"Okay. It's all right. Are you okay? All right.
Where did it happen?"

He raised his head from my shoulder and blinked mistily. "In the john."

I took a deep breath and squared my shoulders.

"You wait here," I said.

I turned and strode back into the Club Wow.

The proprietors of the average Chicago exotic dance club don't subscribe to the credo that the customer is always right.

I tried to emphasize that I wasn't accusing anyone. All I was trying to do was find out who had taken my uncle's baseball card from him in the men's room. But the manager—a heavyset guy with one of those grim, beefy faces—didn't know anything about it, and didn't want to know anything about it, and didn't want me to ask any of the customers about it. He said they were watching the show and didn't want to be disturbed.

So I lost my temper.

"Hey, pal," I said to this guy, who could easily have been Fat Ronnie Buoniconti himself. "That card's a family heirloom, and I'm not leaving here until I find out who took it."

Shows how wrong you can be. As I started toward one of the runway tables to begin my interrogation, I experienced a sensation I hadn't had since I was a kid: being carried. Two of the house employees grasped my upper arms. I found myself changing direction, moving along rapidly, skating over the floor and out the door before I could think of anything except, "This is the bum's rush."

They were actually gentle about it, initially. They just gave me an easy push as we reached the sidewalk. Uncle Rollie was still standing where I'd left him, looking up the street.

I turned and went back in, having thought of a more persuasive way to make my point. I was going to offer them money. But when I reentered, the two guys who'd thrown me out were standing there, just inside the door, and they didn't give me the chance to talk. Seeing me again affronted them. The bigger one grabbed me by my shirtfront. His teeth clenched. His face was red and wider than it was long.

"Asshole," he said.

He head-butted me in the hairline. If he'd hit the spot I'd been butted in already, I think I might've screamed. As it was, I was more surprised than hurt . . . at first. Then he and his partner spun me around and gave me a neck-snapping, four-handed shove, back out the door, across the sidewalk and into a bus-stop sign which I met with my left shoulder and collarbone. After that, I sort of sat down on the curb. Then I thought I'd lie down on it for a minute.

Resting on my back on the pavement, a clammy sweat beginning to cover me, I thought I saw Charlotte's face appear against the sky, looking down at me with an angry, censorious expression. She looked like an angel come down from heaven to slap my face.

I closed my eyes for three slow beats and opened them, satisfying myself that it was really her. Then I raised my hand. She didn't take it. She walked away from me.

I rolled over to see Big Stan Cornell and Billy Garner looking at the posters on display on the building facade. Also examining these photos was Dillon, until Charlotte yanked him away. I slowly came to the realization that she was mad at me for coming out of the Club Wow. Or rather, not so much for coming *out*.

She returned, with Dillon in hand, to stand over me again. She gestured to indicate Uncle Rollie, who was now sitting on the bus-stop bench.

"He's out here, Cooper," she remarked icily.

"Well, but he said the card was in there."

"No, I didn't," said Uncle Rollie.

I stared at him, dazed.

"Dillon, go and sit by Rollie," said Charlotte. "Go on." She waited for him to do so, and then bent down to confide in me.

"Fuck you, Cooper," she murmured.

"Now, wait a minute," I said, struggling to my feet—injured and unaided, I would like to record.

"I hope you're proud of yourself," Charlotte intoned, her voice low but thrumming and throbbing. "You leave your uncle alone on the street so you can go in and drool over a pumped-up boob babe. I won't even mention what you said to me not half an hour ago."

"Hey, hold it. *He* was the one who was drooling."

Charlotte shook her head.

"Put it on an old man."

"*Hey*. He said somebody took the card away

162

from him in the *john*." I made my way woozily over to Uncle Rollie and squatted down in front of him, clutching the bench for support.

"Don't you remember? In the john, you said."

Uncle Rollie nodded slowly. "Not that john, though."

"What?"

He fumbled in his shirt pocket, produced a crumpled piece of paper, and handed it to me. It was a receipt. On top it said "Lee Vivyan Collectibles," with an address in New York. Written across it was "Sold to L. Vivyan, 1909 Schulte, $500," and on the bottom there was a shaky, semi-legible "R. Zerbs."

I looked up from the receipt to R. Zerbs. Each of us waited for the other to tell him what had happened.

This is the story as we got it from Uncle Rollie, out on the curb at the bus stop. He did pretty well on the reconstruction, I think . . . probably because the incident was so much of a shock that it impressed itself, at least temporarily, on his mind.

The exact dialogue and stage business will probably never be known. As supplied by Uncle Rollie it's approximate. I am combining his memory with my memory of what he told me, so it *has* to be approximate. But his version was later verified in essence, so I'm pretty confident in putting it down as follows:

His memory starts in the men's room down the corridor from Hall C at the convention center. He must have gone there right after I left him with Dillon.

We fade in on a row of gleaming sinks.

Lee Vivyan comes in. Uncle Rollie sees him in the mirror over the sinks. There's another man there, too, but he leaves.

Vivyan comes up next to Uncle Rollie, who is drying his hands with a paper towel. Vivyan says he wants another look at the card. Wants to see if it's a fake.

Uncle Rollie is offended at this implication and says, Ain't no fake. He removes the card from his pocket and holds it out. Vivyan takes it carefully and squints at it.

Finally he says, Okay, five hundred dollars.

Five *hundred*? says Uncle Rollie. That don't seem right.

It's right, says Vivyan.

The business here gets a little muddy. Like a magician, Vivyan suddenly has five one-hundred-dollar bills in his hand. The card is gone somehow, nowhere to be seen. He offers the bills to Uncle Rollie.

Uncle Rollie says, We're supposed to have an auction.

Take the money, says Vivyan.

No, gimme my card back.

Vivyan muscles him slightly, saying, Pop, hey listen. You *sold* it. You just sold it to me. Here, see?

He stuffs the cash into Uncle Rollie's shirt pocket.

Now you got money. Okay? You're paid. You sold it. You made a great deal, I didn't want to pay this much, you brought me to my knees.

Again magically, Vivyan is holding a pen and receipt pad. He helps Uncle Rollie write on the pad. The old man struggles ineffectually.

Some kid comes into the room. Vivyan begins readjusting Uncle Rollie's attire, talking encouragingly to him, suggesting that he get some air. Vivyan leaves. The kid finishes peeing and turns to stare at Uncle Rollie, who stares back, bewildered.

Uncle Rollie says, Who are you?

That's the scene as he recalled it out in front of the Club Wow. His next memories after that were of Misty Rue, who, he said, turned out to be from Davenport originally.

When he'd finished, and I'd gotten tired of staring at the receipt in my hand, I looked up at him and apologized again for leaving him alone. Not much good, of course.

He was looking old, blotchy, and saggy. And apprehensive, as he goggled at the pedestrians and traffic going by—a gritty smear of movement and noise surrounding us.

"It didn't use to sound like this," he said.

I stood up slowly, aching inside and out. Charlotte, Dillon, Big Stan and Billy Garner had all heard the story.

"Guy like that dealer," said Billy Garner, "only understands one thing."

"Puts him one up on you," said Charlotte.

"We goin' back there?" asked Big Stan.

"Absolutely," I said.

Charlotte brushed some curb dirt further into my

sleeve. "You all right?" she asked.

"I don't know," I said with dignity, rubbing my shoulder.

"Sorry about that 'fuck you.' "

"Well, you should be. I don't talk to you like that."

"I know."

"You've been very critical today."

"I know."

There was no real fun in seeing her feeling guilty. I had a lot more to feel guilty about.

Everyone looked at me, waiting for the new strategy. I got to thinking of the type of CEO you read about sometimes, who plots the path of his company and leads it straight into bankruptcy, plunging his employees onto the dole, down through the cracks, losing their health insurance and finally their homes. I thought, I could do that.

After some careful experimentation I decided I could travel. We all took a last glance at Misty Rue on the wall and walked away from the Club Wow.

CHAPTER FOURTEEN

Uncle Rollie was a little green around the crust, so we walked slowly to the convention center, stopping briefly at my bank so I could cash my paycheck. Then we all went back in a clump to Hall C and straight to Lee Vivyan's booth. He sat impassively in a folding chair, drinking from a plastic water bottle and waiting for us. His pal Carl wasn't in evidence.

"You've got my uncle's Frank Schulte card," I said to him.

"I bought it," he replied.

"For five hundred dollars?"

Vivyan blinked his eyes once for yes. Mad Dog McClure, standing next door and turning from a commercial, barked an incredulous laugh.

"Five hundred is a joke," he declared flatly.

Vivyan shrugged, leaning back on the rear legs of his chair.

"I can't help it if the old guy's not real sharp

anymore," he said. "That's life. People don't age like fine wine. They age like meat."

I went into my pocket.

"Here's the money back," I said, producing it. "Gimme the card."

"*No*," said Vivyan, clunking forward on his chair, suddenly glaring. "And I'll tell you why. Because you don't deserve it. You hillbillies want to get rich for some piece of paper you found in Grampa's desk? Fuck ya. That card belongs to somebody who can appreciate it."

Having delivered himself of this logical leap, he spoke to Mad Dog McClure, ignoring us.

"Nine out of ten people don't know. They don't know. Guy comes up, shows me a '59 Maris, VG at best, wants one-sixty. I said to him, Let's forget for a minute that you're a moron. You should *give* me that Maris. I saw him play. I know what I saw. You go to the game and only remember you did the fuckin' wave."

He snorted a laugh.

"What in the hell," I asked sincerely, "are you talking about?"

"Ignorance," he said.

I peered at him, searching for meaning.

"You still don't get it?" Vivyan asked.

I shook my head. He snorted again, looking at McClure and pointing a thumb at me in a "get him" gesture.

"I'm not sure I get it either," said Mad Dog.

Vivyan got exasperated.

"Okay. Awright. I'm gonna tell the both of you a little story. Make it clear."

He sat back, planted his plastic water bottle on his thigh, and glowered at me.

"1980," he said. "I'm cold-calling for Excelsior Rare Coin & Bullion. Nothing job. But I know where the cards are going. Everybody says they've already peaked, but I'm putting every nickel into the old ones wherever I can find them. I'm gonna start my old lady and me off in the business. To do this I got to be away from home a lot."

He leaned forward and put the water bottle down.

"One night I come back late and Pauline is standing in the kitchen like Gloria Swanson in *Sunset Boulevard*, eyebrows up to here . . . by a pot of spaghetti sauce. And around the rim of the pot she's balanced half a dozen '50s cards. Mostly commons—the Throneberry brothers, Art Ceccarelli, she didn't know from value—but also a '53 Yogi Berra and a '55 Koufax rookie. Near-Mint.

"Turns out she's pissed at me for ignoring her. Says the only ones get treated like humans at our place are the cards. And all the time she's talking, the steam from the sauce is coming up and warping them. But I can't rush her. She's got a ladle in her hand. She can tip 'em all in the pot: the great and the near-great.

"I can't *believe* it. I can't believe the vicious ignorance. Like they weren't her future, too. On top of that, these cards are from my own private childhood collection. They're like my oldest friends.

"So she stands there and actually says—she *says* this—'People are more important than things.' I tell her, 'These things *are* people, stupid! Beyond that, they're your fuckin' *legacy*!' Whereupon . . . she backhands Yogi Berra right into the pot. He lands faceup on the skin of the sauce and she takes the ladle and *mooshes* him to the bottom. What I mean, brutal."

Vivyan sat back in his chair, brooding darkly at the recollection.

"The Koufax didn't drop. I saved it by convincing her I loved her. I crawled. But I got her later. When we split things up, she got none of it. Because she deserved none of it. She could've had half, but she was too ignorant to appreciate it. She didn't know what she had. At the end I got her . . . for Yogi."

He nodded grimly, then looked up at me.

"Write this down, rube: People who don't know what they got, don't deserve to keep it."

I rummaged through this curious anecdote and finally uncovered the point buried beneath it.

"You *stole* our *card*," I told him. "You got my uncle alone and ripped it out of his hand. I don't want your comical philosophy of who deserves what. You waited, you watched him, and you left your—hey," I said to McClure, "did he leave his booth before?"

"Yeah, he asked me to watch it for him."

"So what?" said Vivyan. "I *bought* it in the men's room. I gave him one of my receipts for a purchase order. I got a copy. Here. He signed it. Here."

"That's not his signature."

"Hell it's not."

"You *made* him sign it. A kid was in there and saw you. The signature doesn't look right. It's not natural."

"Looks good to me. What kid?"

I turned to Mad Dog McClure.

"This treacherous, oily bastard," I said, gesturing at Vivyan, "robbed my uncle. What about it?"

Mad Dog looked pained as he gazed at the receipt in Vivyan's hand. Also, the game was in progress on the overhead TV. He shook his head.

"Hate to say it, but it looks like a court case. Handwriting guys . . . where's this kid who saw it? Kind of thing could take a year or two."

I glanced at Uncle Rollie. If ever there was a man who couldn't wait a year or two, it was him. He wouldn't remember Vivyan at all in a week.

At the moment he seemed groggy. He showed no indication of having heard any of the preceding conversation. In fact, he was showing an inclination to take a little nap right on the spot, although there was nothing under him but the floor. As I stared at him, he sank to the cement, sat down, and slowly, almost imperceptibly, rocked back off his bottom and onto his back, like a big old saggy beetle. He seemed surprised.

I was scared. I joined Charlotte and Big Stan, squatting over him.

"What happened? Can you talk? Can you breathe?" I half shouted at him, supporting his head.

"Are you in pain?" asked Charlotte.

"I think I'm hungry," he said, looking mystified. "Did we eat today?"

"Breakfast and a burger is all. Are you okay?"

"I'm *old*. It's no damn joke." He put his hands up for Big Stan and me to help him up, which we did, carefully.

"He needs a place to sit down and a healthy meal, not junk," said Charlotte.

"I need a new set of legs," he muttered. "Complete new set of joints and organs, I should say. Get 'em out of the Monkey Ward catalogue. What did you say, am I in pain? You'll find out. You walk around and don't even know you're walking, but I know it when *I'm* walking."

Big Stan left me to support Uncle Rollie and moved forward to Lee Vivyan's table. He leaned over it, putting his fists on either side of Joe DiMaggio's shoelaces, and stared menacingly down at the dealer.

"I think you better give back the card you took from this old man," he said.

Lee Vivyan blinked rapidly, surveying Big Stan from his clenched fists up to his clenched expression.

"Shit. Why didn't you say so?" he said.

He leaned forward and reached down, bringing up his gun and resting it on the table, pointed up slightly at Big Stan's belly.

"I don't care how many situps you do," he said.

The flagship Mr. Green Genes salad palace is on Ontario, west of Michigan. It occupies the ground floor of an office building. Its logo, or figurehead, under the name on the front of the door, is a comic-book type splash of personified, muscular celery, carrots, tomatoes, and cucumbers, exploding out of a head of lettuce. There are also happy-face decals of healthy people on the windows, radiating the glow that comes with eating right.

That vegetables are good for you is not, to my knowledge, disputed. Experts recommend carrots and greens more than they do animal fat and ice cream. And the hybrids developed by the Mr. Green Genes technicians are apparently the best that nature and man combined can produce. The promotional challenge from the Mr. Green Genes standpoint is to make them somehow enjoyable to the great mass of citizens. Attractive fast food.

It's my opinion that the Mr. Green Genes people have signally failed to do this. I wouldn't care, except that as they go, so goes Charlotte's painting.

Our crowd went over there in Charlotte's wagon after the confrontation with Lee Vivyan, to get something good for Uncle Rollie to eat and try to think what to do next.

Inside, the walls and booths were shades of yellow and green. Charlotte's painting was up and on display, on the wall in the hallway that led to the restrooms. She didn't care for the location, but didn't grouse about it. She was more concerned about Uncle Rollie, making sure he got the super salad.

We were a glum group in our dark green booth, poking at our genetically toughened fare. Dillon was quieter than ever; he hadn't said a word since Charlotte yelled at him for losing sight of Uncle Rollie at the card show. Uncle Rollie himself was listless and dazed. Big Stan's sympathy for our loss of the card was so profound that each look at his face was a reminder to feel bad.

Billy Garner was finding sobriety to be just about what he might have expected. He took one of the cherry tomatoes off his plate and bounced it experimentally on the floor.

I took Charlotte over to look at her painting. We stood before it as customers went to and from the restrooms behind us.

"It looks good," I said.

"I don't think there'll be many copies," said Charlotte. "I am not optimistic about the future of this chain. How was your corn?"

"It was fresh. They kind of bred the sweetness out of it."

"The broccoli is so springy, your teeth practically bounce off."

"They need some butter or sauce or side of fries or something."

"I'm not going to get rich on this, am I?" she asked.

"Well, you never know. People like healthy things. They might suffer to, you know, live." I cleared my throat. My private opinion was that eating at Mr. Green Genes made you wonder what was the point of going on. But in my present frame of mind I would have felt that way even with prime rib.

"Wish I could help him," she said, looking back

174

toward our booth. I turned to follow her gaze.

Uncle Rollie stared out the window with his hands in his lap. Then he glanced around and did a startled double take at the sight of Big Stan Cornell sitting next to him.

Red Skelton once did a nightmarish pantomime about an astronaut. He was out in the void in his space suit, attached to his rocket ship by a cord. Had a helmet on. And he was floating, out beyond gravity. He did some funny things at first, like Red Skelton would. But then, somehow, the cord broke or came untied, and he was cut loose from the ship. And he screamed, but you couldn't hear him through the helmet. Then he floated slowly away, doomed. The horror in it wasn't so much that he was dying, but that he was disconnected.

"It's been a disaster," I conceded.

"Are you going to the police?"

"He can't wait around for cops and court and who did what. Look at him. He's done. He's gotta go home."

"What home are you referring to?" asked Charlotte.

I stared at him. He had always been larger and more vivid to me than anyone in LaPorte. Now he was visibly dwindling inside my overcoat. Turning away, trying to visualize him in his prime, I found myself eulogizing him in my head.

This was the flamboyant baseball-card donor I looked up to as a boy. . . . the man my mother called King of the Loafers, a title which may not suggest a

dynamic personality but does imply leadership qual-
ities. . . . the man who turned his father's failed tavern
into the mecca of LaPorte drinking society.

John Zerbs had the sound idea to start a basement tap in the pre-air-conditioning days, but he was
financially unfortunate. By the time he died, in 1958,
the place was buried in every way. Uncle Rollie reopened it on his own and kept it open.

He was a man other men gathered around, if
only to get mad. Folks in LaPorte periodically grind
together too close and get bitterly angry at each other;
it's the friction of permanent proximity. But at Uncle
Rollie's tap, enemies would reconcile in their mutual
outrage over, for example, his search for a volunteer
to help him kick off a barfly exchange system with
the Soviets. He was always ready, back then, with a
sporting proposal to raise a dazed face out of its beer
mug.

He once offered a month's free Budweiser to
whoever in town could roll a hoop the farthest. He
handicapped the event for age, and I was one of the
lucky juvenile railbirds who got to see it, on a hot
afternoon nearly thirty years ago. Potbellied men
whose sense of dignity had always forbidden any sudden movement lurched in zigzags all over Front Street
in the summer sun, chasing their hoops with stick in
hand, while Uncle Rollie acted as steward from the
shade of a diner awning. I have a near-mint mental
picture of him in a Lincolnian posture, overseeing
everyone with quiet satisfaction. His customers considered him a fool to give away all that beer to the

winner, but he stood there that day as if it was worth it.

He seemed to get more enjoyment from life than the Upper Bluff adults who were held up to me as better examples. He used to drive through town in unmarried splendor with Linda Joy Ballinger, another extrovert, in his truck on the way to Quincy, and the Tyke side of the family would just seethe. Maybe he was smiling to cover a broken heart over Mom.

After Linda Joy died one night with another man in a wreck on the old two-lane road between LaPorte and Stallard, Uncle Rollie settled into more sedate arrangements, ending with Callie McAllister. He never headed up a formal family, just the bar. If he had regrets about this as he got older, he channeled them into his business, and his fish. He said the fish satisfied his longing for unpredictable conversation.

Selling the tap and losing his customers may have made him a little overly dependent on those fish; an ex-barman may need company more than most.

Looking at him now in the Mr. Green Genes restaurant, I could see that short of proprietorship of another establishment, his only remaining source of independent comfort and society lay in his ratty old house and the river. Away from there, he rapidly shrank.

On the other hand, he needed a caretaker in that ratty old house, and at least partially thanks to me, he couldn't afford one. So what about it?

Earlier in the day, when Charlotte had accused me of avoiding anything tough, she'd been more right than I wanted her to be. My own version of diminished capacity, in recent months, had extended to the heart.

It wasn't that I had stayed home instead of mountain climbing or skydiving. I wouldn't do those things anytime. It was more that I'd insulated myself from difficulty . . . from people with their demands, dilemmas, and mess. I had preferred, on the whole, the company of characters in old movies. People who didn't have to be cleaned up after or paid attention to.

But Uncle Rollie clearly wasn't the kind of person you could love from a distance anymore.

One trait I believe I inherited from my dad is that I generally *will* do the right thing if I'm cornered. When Dad found out he was dying, he became an attentive parent and would have been a loving husband if it hadn't been way too late.

Faced with a financial catastrophe, and the prospect of leaving Uncle Rollie to professionals, I made my decision.

"I'll go back with him," I told Charlotte as we stood before her painting. "I'll stay with him. We can burn down the house together."

"In *LaPorte*? What are you gonna do for work?"

"De-tassel corn, I don't know."

She looked anxiously into my eyes to see if I'd lost my mind.

"Cooper, that's a fine gesture, but you all need money. You need that card."

"Well, yeah. But how to get it. The only way I

can think of, I'd end up on the news with the an-
chorman saying, 'Cornered by police, Zerbs then
turned the gun on himself.' "

There was a commotion over where they take
your order. We turned to see Dillon, red-faced in his
Cardinals cap, hollering up at the counterboy.

"You put my mom's picture someplace better!"

"I'm sorry?"

"She should be up in the window or on that wall
instead of by the bathroom! My mom did that picture! It's not supposed to be by the bathroom! It's
better'n that piece of crap you got in the window!"

"Do we have a parent here for this kid?"

"Right here," said Charlotte. "C'mon, Dill."

Dillon was in tears, resisting her efforts to pull
him back to the booth.

"They got you next to the bathroom, Mom!"

"Could've been worse, hon. They could've put it
over the grill."

"We don't have a grill," said the counterboy, a
well-built, well-coached kid. "All our food is fresh
and raw, with the nutrients locked in."

Dillon was crying openly now, and surrendered
to Charlotte's hug as she walked him back to our
booth.

"We thought he was going to the toilet," said Big
Stan.

"I'm sorry," Dillon said.

"What for, honey?"

"I didn't watch him," he said, looking at Uncle
Rollie. "I forgot."

I squatted in front of the boy as he sat down. "Dillon, I can out-forget you the best day you ever saw. That wasn't your fault. That was my job. Don't worry about that."

"Nobody's mad at you, hon," Charlotte told him. "Have some more salad."

"No, that's okay," he said.

"They put your mom's picture where they did," I said, "so everybody would see it. Because everybody's gotta go sometime. That's like . . . marketing. They do that at the Art Institute. All the best stuff's right near the restroom."

Dillon sighed. After a moment his features relaxed slightly under the bill of his cap. He glanced once back at the counterboy.

"If I was Wolverine I woulda sliced that guy in five slices," he said wistfully.

Charlotte and I sat on either side of him in the booth. He rested his head on her shoulder.

"Loren, where in the hell are we?" asked Uncle Rollie across the table.

"We're in Chicago, and I'm Cooper."

"What did *I* say?"

"What about the card?" said Billy Garner. "Are we just givin' up on that?"

I glared at him.

"Hey," I told him. "You sitting with us in no way means we are partners or pals, Billy. You shot my dog right off my bookcase."

"Yeah?" Billy snarled. "You think you're so goddamn special with your Chicago apartment. Know what I think of people like you?"

And he swept his plate onto the floor. Just back-handed it into the aisle, like Jack Nicholson in one of his old tantrums.

"*Geez*," said Dillon.

"That's good, Billy," said Charlotte.

"That's it," I said. "This guy isn't a relative, he isn't a friend. As far as I'm concerned, he can be re-placed."

"Hey, I don't care," said Billy. "I hate ch'all. I don't give a shit." His eyes suddenly overflowed with tears as the counterboy came over to see what the trouble was.

"Treat me like an asshole . . ." Billy went on. "I'm not an asshole, I'm *sick*."

"You could be both," I suggested.

"He's trying, Cooper," said Stan. "The first day is tough. It's a twelve-step program and he's on step one here."

"Oh, bullshit. You don't know anything about me," Billy said to him. "I'm not even an alcoholic. I'm complex, is all."

"I don't care how complex you are, you can be-have in a restaurant or I'll pop you like a zit," Stan informed him.

Billy had no comment to make to this.

"Pick up your plate," said Big Stan.

Billy got up to assist the counterboy.

"He brought up a point, you know," Stan said to me. "What *about* the card? You want me to jump that Lee Vivyan when he leaves the show?"

"Nah. He'd shoot you."

I rubbed my temples, feeling that old pressure. I had no ideas.

Wildfire Schulte. Wildfire Schulte. The name seemed fictional, nonsensical to me. So did the money we'd thought to get for this "Wildfire Schulte" baseball card. Why should anybody, after all, care? Nobody remembered this Schulte character. The card itself was becoming hazy and dreamlike in my mind's eye.

"You know, I can't even remember what the card looks like."

"Well, I can help you on that. It looks like this," said Big Stan.

And he pulled this card out of his wallet.

It goes to show how each event had been blotting out the one before. Not only had I forgotten asking Dee Francona to make that facsimile card—no surprise there, really—but Big Stan had forgotten, too. He'd meant to give it to me as soon as he got to the show, but what with Uncle Rollie vanishing, it had slipped his mind.

Dee had gone ahead and done a rush job for me as soon as he heard I was getting kicked out of the Times Building. He'd done it on thin art board, and it looked good considering how little time he'd had. It actually resembled the original, although it clearly wasn't eighty-five years old. He'd returned the snapshot with it so I could compare.

Charlotte looked at the two Schultes over my shoulder.

"He missed on the mouth," she said. "I think I could fix it."

At first, there was a frustrating feeling in my head . . . a feeling of vacancy, of a section of ground lying fallow. This facsimile card, I sensed, was supposed to be a stimulus. Seeing it, I realized it should give me an idea, but I didn't know what the idea it was supposed to give me.

Then slowly, something began budding, pushing, timidly at first, up through the dried-out mental mulch inside my skull. Something pulsated and throbbed in my brain. I felt a feverish heat on my face. Something was coming forth.

"The trouble with me," I said softly, "is my attitude. I look for weaknesses in this Lee Vivyan, and I don't see any. *We've* got all the weaknesses. And he's got us down. He's got the card. His foot is on our throat. But you know what it's like?"

I held up Dee Francona's artwork.

"It's like the comics. No, listen. I edited those things a long time. They do some mean things in those strips, you know. Day after day. Cavewomen take full-grown snakes and whap their brains out on rocks. Cockney layabouts roll down the street in a cloud of dust with stars coming out of it, punching their wives. I've seen people squashed, split in two, bludgeoned, impaled . . ."

I stopped, completely adrift, and shook my head.

"Wow. I'm sorry. I completely lost the thread. Boy. . . . No, wait. Here it is. Looking at all that, I learned something: You can come back. There's always another strip. You're not through till you're whited out."

They stared at me, uncomprehending. But I didn't care. The bud had bloomed.

"Don't you get it? What if we *are* alcoholics? What if we *are* mentally impaired, and too old, and too young, and weaker, and unarmed, and unemployed? We can come back anyway. We can *beat* him! We can take all our weaknesses and put them together into one gigantic . . . no. We can take all our weaknesses and put them *aside*. How about it? Are you with me?"

The counterboy was.

"Excuse me," he said, "but do you people act like this at home? We just opened, you know."

I noticed that I had risen and was blocking the aisle. People from other booths were staring. I raised a hand and reached for my wallet.

"Never mind, kid, we were leaving anyway. Here, juice for everybody; we're celebrating. Cooper Zerbs got an idea."

CHAPTER FIFTEEN

It was closing time. People were leaving Hall C. Maintenance men were mopping the floor.

I stood two aisles down from Lee Vivyan's corner booth, waiting behind a Negro Leagues display. I could see him in his folding chair. He was laughing, watching Mad Dog McClure.

Up on the overhanging TVs, the Cub-Dodger game had just ended. The Cubs had led going into the ninth, but a pitching change with men on base hadn't worked out. The playoffs were over. And although Mad Dog had seen it coming, he was taking it hard. He was at the climax of a stomping, cursing, howling fit up and down his aisle, Aisle J, showing that there was, after all, a story behind his nickname. His wife watched sympathetically as he smashed a Walkman blaster on the floor in front of their booth. Then he jumped up and down on it, finally kicking the biggest remaining piece across aisles J and K.

"Fuckin' *percentages*! Lefty-lefty! Righty-righty! How 'bout acquiring some fucking BALLS and pitching the best fuckin' PITCHER! How can you let your season come down to Fleming? How can you depend on fuckin' straight fastball hanging curve asshole *Fleming* with the season on the line? Can you explain that to me? Was that the *percentage* move? Hey, here's a percentage: IT DIDN'T WORK! THE SEASON'S OVER! It's one hundred PERCENT OVER! Here's how many fucking *percent* that move has worked in the last game of the playoffs: *NEVER!*"

Everyone still in the hall was watching him, of course, although a few had to turn away. An older, uniformed Security guy came over toward Mad Dog, but Diane McClure intercepted him and said, "It's all right. He's almost done. He's just so unhappy. He'll clean it all up."

And it was true; he was winding down. A few more kicks, some flailing spins, some sobs ripped from his chest and throat, and he was standing there, breathing deeply, eyes closed. Finally, his eyes opened again. His wife handed him a Hefty bag. He began picking up the pieces.

"Well," he said softly, his voice cracking, "they did it again."

A minute or so later a couple of well-dressed, middle-aged men came up to him. They were both heavyset, with reddish faces, but one of them had this great white hair, combed so it waved, and the other one had nothing to comb. The white-haired one said something to Mad Dog and they both shook hands

with him. I couldn't hear the visitors, but I could hear
McClure:

"I may bid on it myself," he said, breathing heavily and stabbing a forefinger at the TV. "I'm not going
to let that team kill me."

He bent down to pick up another piece of debris,
then straightened again.

"I used to think," he went on, "when they'd lose
like that, y'know: Cut me open, pour in the gasoline,
and drop the match. But I refuse to do it anymore. *I
will no longer identify with that ball club.* From now
on, I equate myself with the *1908* ball club. That team
will never let me down. From now on I root for the
1908 Cubs. I think we have a very good chance of
beating Detroit in the Series."

The three of them walked over to Lee Vivyan's
booth. Vivyan was still sitting back in his folding
chair. The only other guy there was Carl, the short,
muscular, ponytailed representative of Fat Ronnie
Buoniconti.

Mad Dog introduced the two well-dressed men
to Vivyan. I couldn't hear them, but I didn't want to
get any closer yet. I was waiting for an indication that
the card was still there.

But Vivyan didn't move off his chair. He just sat
while the white-haired man talked. Then he started
shaking his head and talking back, and I decided I
had to implement the Plan.

I went back toward the entrance, to my group.
Charlotte, Uncle Rollie, Big Stan, Billy Garner, and
Dillon were over by the long promotional giveaway

table. Charlotte had found Uncle Rollie a folding chair and the others were standing.

"I can't tell if it's there or not," I said.

"Okay, we'll go up—" said Charlotte.

"First, *I'll* go up. Then I'll signal you, and then you and Uncle Rollie go up, past me."

"Right, and we'll say we've—"

"No, *he'll* say—"

"Okay, *he'll* say his line."

"Uncle Rollie, do you know your line?"

"When are we goin' home?" he asked.

"No. Work with him on his line."

"He's tired, Cooper."

I squatted down in front of him.

"Uncle Rollie, I've got an idea for getting your card back. You just have to say one thing. Charlotte's gonna work with you on it. I know you're tired. Let's just try this one idea, and then we'll go home. Win or lose. Okay?"

Uncle Rollie gave me a little smile.

"Wish I had a scooter," he said.

But he insisted he was up to it, and I turned to Big Stan.

"Vivyan's got that corner booth, so you go up Aisle J and I'll come up the other side. If something stupid has to be done, let me do it."

He agreed, and we all fanned out.

This time I circled around, came up Aisle 5 to the booth two shy of Vivyan's, and peered past a poster of the Raiderettes. Mad Dog saw me, but said nothing when I gestured downwards with both hands. I could hear Vivyan now.

"I don't care. I'm not showing it. Formal auction. That's where you'll see it. You want to register for the auction, fine."

"We'd like a look at the card," said the bald one. Vivyan shrugged.

"You're not gonna look at it today," he said.

I turned and waved Charlotte and Uncle Rollie on. As they walked past me, she winked and gave me a pat on the ass.

She was more confident than I was. The whole thing was my idea, and just because I'd finally had an idea didn't make it a good one. Standing behind the Raiderettes poster and waiting to make my big move, I suddenly saw several areas in which it came up flimsy. I realized I hadn't thought it through very well. I had no contingency plan. Nor did I have a long-term plan in case of an initial favorable outcome. If I'd had the time I'd have called everyone back for further discussion.

But we were on. Uncle Rollie walked up to Mad Dog's two visitors, waved our duplicate Schulte card at them, and said, "This here's the real one." That was his line, and he delivered it with spirit and brio, word perfect.

My eyes were on Lee Vivyan, and I saw him re-act, giving up his poker face for a dumbfounded look I found gratifying.

While Mad Dog and the two collectors trans-ferred their attention to Uncle Rollie, Vivyan clomped

to the floor on his chair, stood up, and leaned forward
to peer at Uncle Rollie's hand.

"Bullshit," he said.

Charlotte took the card from Uncle Rollie. She
was careful to keep it out from under everyone's nose;
despite the touch-up she'd given it, it still wouldn't
hold up five seconds under a close look.

"Sorry," she said sweetly to Vivyan. "The card
you stole from this elderly man was a fake."

"Bullshit," repeated Vivyan, squinting at our version.

"I wouldn't sell it ordinarily," said Uncle Rollie
expansively, "but sometimes you need to liquefy."
This was an ad-lib or embroidery. He seemed to have
revived in performance.

"Frank Patterson and Nelson McCormick," said
Mad Dog to Charlotte, indicating White Hair and
Baldy in turn, "are here to bid on the card."

"Wherever it is," said Patterson.

"There's a Patterson family plot," Uncle Rollie
announced, "next to the Zerbs plot in the LaPorte
cemetery."

This was received in silence until Charlotte
warned Patterson, "Now don't take advantage of the
acquaintaince." Then she gave a laugh I would have
to call coquettish. I hadn't heard her do one since high
school.

The ponytailed man Carl moved up to Lee Vivyan and murmured something I couldn't make out. It
acted on Vivyan like a poke with a stick. He flinched,

shook his head, and kept staring across at the card in Charlotte's hand.

McCormick presented his palm to Charlotte, asking to see the card, and Charlotte made a show of asking Uncle Rollie whether it was all right with him. Pretty soon *somebody* was going to get a good view of it, and then we'd be laughed out of the building.

Finally, Vivyan moved. He was standing inside the angle formed by his two display tables. He now took two steps over to the end of the table on my aisle, reached down and unobtrusively took a cassette holder from a small crate of tapes on the floor.

That was my cue. It was as far as my plan went, really. And as far as it went, it had succeeded. Now we were in the improvisational part.

I bolted forward like a running back, reached out going by, and grabbed the cassette holder out of his hand.

Or rather, not quite out of his hand. I got it; I got a grip on it, and he was surprised. But he didn't lose his hold. He wouldn't let go. I swung to a stop and we grappled over it, over the display table.

"Let go, asshole, I'll kill ya," Vivyan snarled, yanking at it. "Look at this, you're disrupting every-thing on the . . . all right." He reached downward and to his right with his free hand.

"Stan!" I yelled. I meant it for a roar, but my voice cracked.

Big Stan came around the corner, stretched over the table, reached under it, and got the pistol. Vivyan and I continued fighting furiously for the cassette holder, cursing, hauling each other back and forth over the table, swinging at each other's faces and slapping at each other's hands.

We drew the remainder of the crowd, including the middle-aged Merkel Security guard who'd come up earlier to check on Mad Dog.

"Easy there," said this uniform. "What's goin' on?"

We subsided a bit, leaning our forearms on the table, glaring at each other over the holder, breathing heavily, neither about to let go.

"Guy's a fuckin' *thief*," said Lee Vivyan.

"*You* are," I said.

The security man looked over my shoulder.

His eyebrows rose. "Are those old Perry Como tapes *valuable*?" he asked. " 'Cause I got the 'It's Impossible' one."

"The card in*side*, Einstein," said Lee Vivyan. "This guy's tryin' to steal my fuckin' *card*."

"My uncle's fuckin' card," I corrected him.

We were each propped on our elbows, gripping the holder identically, our thumbs on top. During the pause that followed, I heard Patterson, the collector, on my left, saying, "Well, *that* one's a fraud."

I twisted my head to see him looking disdainfully down at our own version of Wildfire Schulte in Charlotte's hand.

"I'd be surprised if it's a day old," he said to McCormick.

"Actually," said Charlotte, putting the facsimile back in Uncle Rollie's shirt pocket, "it's not."

"The real card's in here," I said, yanking on the holder. "And it's my uncle's."

"It's mine," said Vivyan. "Somebody shoot him."

"You boys pull too hard on that thing and you might wreck what's inside," remarked Mad Dog Mc-Clure.

"Let go," said Vivyan.

I laughed at him.

I could feel the lid working loose, though, and I was worried about the contents. I didn't want one of those ironic resolutions where we each got a torn half of nothing.

"How about this, Lee?" suggested McClure. "Lee. Hey. You come out from your side, and the both of you walk over here."

McClure pointed across the aisle at a table which had been cleared off by a departing dealer.

"It's not like everybody's gonna blow away, Lee. You gotta see if the card's all right. You can hold on. C'mon. C'mon."

Vivyan didn't like it. But I wasn't letting go, and he couldn't stay propped on his elbows forever. He was literally in an awkward position. So, maintaining his grip on his half of the "Best of Perry Como" cassette holder, he straightened up somewhat and inched sideways to the end of his table. I accompanied him, on my side, and pivoted. Then we walked sideways across the aisle, as if we were carrying a cabinet.

Joining us around the new table were Patterson, McCormick, Mad Dog and Diane McClure, Uncle

Rollie, Charlotte, Dillon, Big Stan, Billy Garner, Carl, Security, and everybody else who was still on the floor. Maybe one hundred people altogether.

Lee Vivyan and I faced each other across the width of the table, our arms extended, the cassette holder suspended over the tabletop. Since we were joined so closely, I had a chance to study him a little bit. He was substantial, all right. His forearms were twice as big around as mine. But he had sweat on his forehead, and under his thinning hair. His dark eyes were a little bloodshot. He had a small whitehead just above his mustache, under his right nostril.

As for me . . . well, the Zerbses don't run to heft. I had seen myself in the men's room mirror a few minutes before and I was skinny from the neck down and discolored from the neck up.

Vivyan blew an abrupt burst of air through his mustache.

"I need to open it up," he said.

"Go ahead."

I grasped his right wrist first, then his left. Now he held the holder but I held him.

He carefully flicked the holder lid off. Wildfire was inside, in his little plastic sleeve.

I got ticked off all over again.

"That card's been in my family since 1909," I said.

"So's your shirt," said Vivyan.

While I tried to improve upon "Oh, yeah?" and "Up yours" as comebacks, Nelson McCormick, the bald collector, muscled his way through the spectators

194

on my right to stand beside me. Frank Patterson was across from him, on Vivyan's left. They looked down on the card, dazzled.

"God almighty," murmured Patterson. "It's Near-Mint."

"It's pristine," said Mad Dog McClure from the end of the table.

"But whose is it?" asked McCormick.

Vivyan and I disagreed on this point. He invoked his receipt and I said the receipt wasn't worth snot.

"Well," said Patterson to Lee Vivyan, "you can forget about your auction. Nobody's going to bid on it while there's a dispute over . . ."

"Why don't you agree to co-ownership?" suggested McCormick.

Vivyan and I saw eye-to-eye on this proposal. We both hated it.

Security said, "Might be best to have the card impounded till you can settle it in court."

Vivyan and I liked this one even less. He actually snarled at Security. I growled a bit myself.

"No court," I said. "No impound. This is my uncle's card and he doesn't have forever to sell it."

"No court, no impound, no uncle and no you," said Vivyan to me. "It's mine."

We weren't getting anywhere. Everybody was looking at everybody else. It seemed to me that sooner or later some uniformed personnel would whap our fingers until we let go and take the card away, and then someday we'd go to court. Only by then Uncle Rollie wouldn't have anything to testify to.

I didn't think Lee Vivyan could wait for a settlement either. He owed money to Fat Ronnie Buoniconti. I'd never heard of Fat Ronnie Buoniconti, but his name had an imposing, unforgiving, no-extensions sound to it.

I pictured the card eventually going to the state of Illinois.

Vivyan had to be thinking along the same lines, because at this point he shook his head.

"I can't believe it," he said.

Fat Ronnie's representative Carl spoke up softly from down the table a bit.

"Jump ball, huh, Lee?"

The sweat became more visible on Vivyan's forehead.

I looked up at Charlotte, hoping she might have an idea that had escaped me. But she shrugged and shook her head.

Security said, "Well . . ."

"Wait a minute," said Mad Dog McClure. "You could do like I saw 'em do in New York once, after a show in Queens. Saw 'em do it over a '52 Mantle."

"Do what?" asked Charlotte.

"Fight it out," said Mad Dog.

Vivyan and I looked at each other with new interest.

"Fight it out how?" asked Security.

"Collector's rules," said Mad Dog.

I stared up at him.

"Beg pardon?"

"Collector's rules," Mad Dog repeated. "No interference. No firearms. We set the card in front of you both, like a face-off. Then you go at it till one of you gives. Man with the card at the end owns it."

We all thought that over.

"What if the card gets damaged?" I asked.

"You got to be careful," said Mad Dog.

Everybody thought *that* over.

Billy Garner said, "Why doesn't somebody hold the card for them while they—"

"Nobody holds the card," said Lee Vivyan and I in near-unison.

"Isn't that kind of primitive?" Charlotte asked Mad Dog.

"Well, it's speedy. And these boys don't want to go to court."

"I think I ought to take the card," said Merkel Security.

"Look," said Mad Dog. "These guys want to settle this today. Let 'em duke it, it'll be over in a couple minutes. There's too much litigation in this society. Besides, to get the card you'd probably have to shoot 'em anyway. Whaddya say? Is this Chicago or not? Could be a good fight, *you* don't know."

There was a moment of silence while we all considered it.

"I could get canned," said Security.

"Tell you what," said Frank Patterson of the wavy white hair. "It's worth it to us"—he indicated McCormick—"to get this thing resolved. It's your decision. If you're worried about your job, I could use a man with initiative over at UniSysTech."

"If it comes to that, I can use one in the TRM building," said McCormick.

Carl, Fat Ronnie's spokesman, now spoke up softly.

"Show's over anyway," he murmured to Security, showing him a bill. "Nobody's asking you to let 'em steal. Just let 'em work it out, man to man. This is in the American tradition."

Security wasn't used to getting business cards, job offers, and hundred-dollar bills shoved at him. He looked around. There was nothing going on. The maintenance crew was out with some suds buckets and that was it. A voice I couldn't identify in the crowd around us said, "C'mon, let 'em do it." Security finally let his eyebrows go up and down once.

"Somebody oughta ref," he said.

"I've had experience," said Carl.

"No," I said.

"How about you?" Security asked Mad Dog. "You're the one with the collector's rules."

"If I'm acceptable to both parties."

"Ahh, he's a schmuck," said Lee Vivyan. "Cub fan. The loser's friend."

"Watch it," said McClure evenly. "I'll knock you out myself."

Vivyan and McClure looked at each other for a moment. Then Vivyan shrugged.

"Fuck it," he said. "He can count to a hundred. He can say, 'This man's dead.' He's fine. Right, Alfalfa?"

This last question was addressed to me, and I

said that McClure was acceptable.

Mad Dog took over then, moving the spectators back from the table and persuading us to let him place the card, in its sleeve, between us, like a puck.

Big Stan, Uncle Rollie, and Charlotte came up to me for a last word.

"Let me substitute, Cooper," said Big Stan.

"Not unless I get my gun back," said Lee Vivyan emphatically.

"Sorry, Stan," I said. "If I thought I could get a favorable ruling on it . . ."

"Cooper, that guy's too big for you," Charlotte muttered. "He's too bulky. His arms are like your legs."

"Well, I'm hoping I've learned something from the beatings I've been taking all day."

She looked at me, anxious.

"Are you doing this because of what I said about you not doing anything tough?"

"No, I said I'd live with Uncle Rollie because of what you said about me not doing anything tough. I'm doing *this* because I got so burned up at this egg-snatcher, I'm hoping to stay mad enough to survive the fight."

Uncle Rollie looked uneasy.

"What's the matter?" I asked him.

"I ain't seen you win ever," he said.

"Well, maybe you've got some ingenious brain-storm on how else we can get it back," I said, annoyed.

"No."

"Any advice?"

"I think you oughta watch you don't bend it."

An intriguing tactical point. We weren't just going to fight. We were going to fight over the card. Literally. As Mad Dog McClure had said, we had to be careful.

Charlotte whispered in my ear.

"Grab it and run."

"Run? Don't you think I can beat him?"

"He's bigger, he's meaner, and no, I don't. That's nothing against you. He's got a killer instinct."

"How can you tell?"

"Wake up, Cooper. *Look* at him."

I did. Vivyan's face wore a dull-eyed, wanted-poster expression.

"I'm gonna castrate you," he said.

"Nice going, smart guy, you just gave away your strategy," I told him.

"Easy, Cooper," said Charlotte.

"Oh, I'm tired of his browbeating bullshit. Vivien Leigh," I chanted at him. "Vivian Vance. Olivia de Havilland, ya big sissy."

Lee Vivyan's eyes widened and his head quivered.

"Cooper, have you lost your mind?" hissed Charlotte.

"He's a thumbsucker," I said. "He covers his eyes at the scary parts."

Vivyan's eyes narrowed.

"All right," he said, nodding. "I get it. I'm not gonna get mad. I'll get the card first, *then* I'll do you."

"You two gentlemen ready?" asked Mad Dog McClure.

Wildfire Schulte, in his soft plastic sleeve, smiled genially up at us.

"I'd like you to remember," Mad Dog said, "what you're fighting for here, and act accordingly."

CHAPTER SIXTEEN

Here's something I've found: Sometimes, during stressful, testing moments, clichés and dead metaphors come to life and regain their power, taking on literal meaning. In this case the one I'm thinking of is "taking your lumps."

I was breaking out in lumps going into this fight. It was astounding to me that I could be preparing for another physical confrontation on a day when all I'd done was ricochet from one to another.

The Zerbses, as a rule, shun violence. I lost interest in fighting by the time I entered high school. Between then and Big Stan, I had no altercations. Then, bam, bam, bam: first Stan, then the kids in the alley, then the bouncer outside the Club Wow, and now this. Without intending to, I'd become a brawler. Worse, I'd become a losing brawler. A canvasback. Going into this one I was 0 and 3.

This one was the big one, though. I could see

that. It was a crucial turning point for Uncle Rollie and for me.

The night before the day my dad died, I was sitting by his bed and he began to weep, silently. He'd been in pain and I started up to get the nurse, but he said, no, he didn't want the nurse. So I sat back down and two tears leaked out of his eyes. I asked him what was wrong, but for the longest time he wouldn't say. Finally he blurted, "I always thought I'd do something."

My dad had had potential. My mother, and probably others—teachers and so on—had told him so. And I'm sure he knew it. But what with one drink after another he destroyed his body before he could reach any kind of stardom. And so as he lay there, beginning to suspect he was dying, he couldn't look back on anything he'd achieved to make it more bearable. Beyond being in pain, he was so unhappy and disappointed in himself.

I said to him on that occasion, "Well, you had me."

"You never did anything either," he said. Then he coughed a laugh. I later realized that this had been a variation on an "egotist" joke he used to like. (Guy 1: I haven't got any friends. Guy 2, his faithful pal: What about me? Guy 1: You probably haven't got any either.)

Gradually he settled down some. He went back to repeating, "Shit," which he had been saying at intervals all day, from the pain.

About a minute later he said, "Maybe you'll do something."

That possibility seemed to comfort him slightly.

We all have our own definition of what constitutes "something." When I was a young man I thought I'd accomplish something in the city. But now, as I stared across the table at Lee Vivyan and riffled back through my accessible memory, I had to agree with Dad: I couldn't find anything I'd done yet, either. I had processed paper competently for several years, but I didn't think that was what he'd been talking about.

This would be a something, though. I was pretty sure my dad would think so. If I got the card back. Then, when I was dying, and always assuming I could remember the incident, I'd be able to say, at least, "I got the goddamn card back." Did something for the family.

And so I prepared myself mentally as well as I could to take some more lumps for the Zerbses. I told myself I wouldn't quit.

This fight was unlike any I've been in or seen, in that it featured a unique counterpoint between brutality and delicacy. When Mad Dog McClure softly said, "Ding," to signal the start, both Vivyan and I grabbed for the card . . . but daintily. We touched fingers and the card simultaneously, and we each recoiled as though the other's hand was afire. We even said, "Agh!" The card slid slightly to the side—his left, my right. I quickly, gingerly shot my hand back

205

out and pulled it toward me, to the edge of the table. Then I picked it up with a smile of triumph, and Vivyan came around the table and punched me in the face.

I kept my right arm up, holding the card gently, as I crashed to the floor.

Vivyan would have jumped on me, maybe, but he was afraid he'd damage the card. So he settled for kicking me. I rolled and got up, keeping the card before me.

This fight demanded an innovative strategy. If one of these cards was introduced into a heavyweight title bout—well, the fighters would probably go ahead and mash it. Those guys are worth more than the card. But for Lee Vivyan and me . . . we valued the Schulte even more than we hated each other. It affected our tactics.

Grasping the prize too hard would ruin it. Holding it at all was a disadvantage. It had by now dawned on me that as long as I held the card, Vivyan had an extra hand free and could hammer me at will. He knew it, too. He was hopping and dancing with excitement and eagerness.

As I rose from the floor, hearing Charlotte call out, "Run, *run*!" he came trotting around to slug me again. As his fist started toward me, I held the card up in front of my face.

It stymied him. He froze in mid-slug, momentarily baffled. And while he did, I was able to land my first punch of the day, on anybody. It was just a left jab under his eye, but it snapped his head back and improved my spirits. I heard Big Stan say, "Yeah!"

Vivyan and I disengaged and circled, feinting, cautious. He was less cocky now, worried about the card.

As we moved counterclockwise, I heard McCormick and Patterson discussing hypothetical damage and intrinsic value. Mad Dog McClure moved with us, in a wider orbit, solemn and attentive. Then Vivyan took the offensive again.

I remember Neville Brand as a psychotic thug in an old Edmond O'Brien movie, maybe *D.O.A.* During the middle part of the picture he kept hitting O'Brien in the stomach and saying, with a chortle, "He don't like it in the belly."

But when it comes to that, how many of us do? When Lee Vivyan found himself prevented by the card from hitting me in the face, he stepped in and put one in my midsection, and I'm here to tell you I didn't like it in the belly, either.

I didn't lose hold of the card, though. Although it was a hindrance equivalent to tying one hand behind my back, I was afraid to put it down. I couldn't think of a safe place to put it. According to Mad Dog, collector's rules forbade handing it off to a friend or relative.

It occurred to me to hand it to Vivyan and let *him* fight one-handed for a while. But . . . I *had* it. I'd gotten it back. Here it had been lost, seemingly forever, and I'd recovered it. If I could only avoid getting beaten senseless, it was ours.

I retreated slowly, hunched over and ducking, the

spectators making room for me, until I bumped into Vivyan's display table. There I took a punch on the forehead, on one of my previous bumps. It hurt so much I got to swearing pretty bad. Then I tried my jab again and somehow got it through, to his nose.

His weakness, I guess. He had a glass beak. He didn't like it in the nose. His eyes filled with water, and he got infuriated. He was just beside himself. I was surprised; he evidently had a low pain threshold. But he didn't want to quit. He seemed to be one of these guys who just gets madder and madder in a fight until he wins or gets knocked out. He started looking around for a weapon. Finally he reached down and grabbed one of Joe DiMaggio's shoelaces from his table.

I didn't think much of his chances of flogging me into submission with a shoelace. I sent another left at him, but he sidestepped it and got behind me. Then he brought the lace over my head and commenced strangling me with it.

"Drop it," he said. "Put it on the floor."

It was serious. I couldn't get my fingers in between the shoelace and the skin of my neck. It burned like crazy, but I stopped worrying about the burning when I couldn't get any wind. I bucked, and elbowed him with my free arm, but it didn't make any difference. He just pulled harder.

"He's killing him!" Charlotte shrieked at Mad Dog McClure. "That's a foul!"

"He said no firearms," Carl pointed out. "He didn't say anything about shoelaces."

"He's *strangling* him," said Big Stan. "That can't be right."

Had I been able to contribute to this discussion, I would've said that Vivyan had introduced a foreign collectible into the fight, and that he should be disqualified.

But it began to look as though the controversy was going to be settled against me. No matter how I shook and danced, I couldn't get Lee Vivyan off. He rode me down to my forearms and knees.

I couldn't breathe. All I could see was the card, in my fingers, against the cement floor. Everything else in me was throttled and straining. My fingers were shaking with the effort to hold it gently.

I had obviously screwed up. I had played it wrong.

Somebody was saying, "Let go," in my ear. It was Vivyan at first, but then it didn't sound like him anymore. The voice still said, "Let go," but it wasn't his. It was Uncle Rollie's.

He was kneeling beside me, so I could see him in my pop-eyed peripheral vision. His face was huge. He looked worried and sad.

"It's all right, boy. Let go. Don't do it anymore."

He was letting me off the hook.

Then I lost sight of him.

I don't know if it was one of those out-of-body experiences. If so it was very brief, and not serene. There wasn't any shining corridor with a warm bright light. It was more like the disorientation and identity-splitting you experience as your mind melts into or out of a dream. The incidents of my life didn't pass before me. But I got a kind of overview.

I was looking down, seeing myself from outside and above. The Cooper below, on his forearms and knees, looked pathetic and foolish. I was ashamed of him. I had let him lose direction. Only a drifting, rudderless person would allow himself to get into a situation like this. No person who had command of his own life would be vulnerable to a set of circumstances that would culminate in his getting strangled by one of Joe DiMaggio's shoelaces.

It was becoming confusing to me. I was dying, and it all had to do with this card in my hand. Everybody wanted me to drop it, and I didn't want to. I was being stubborn about it.

It showed that you can't predict what will finally get you. All the advice I'd ever listened to had turned out to be superfluous. All the talk about red meat and alcohol, saturated fat and women with problems. I might as well have carried on like Henry VIII or Dad. At the end, I was regretting what I hadn't done, not what I had.

I regretted not having kept up correspondence with my friends from Culver-Polk Junior College. You intend to write. After you realize you're not going to write, you intend to phone. I wondered what they'd think when they read the circumstances of my death in the alumni bulletin.

Charlotte was hollering at me. She'd been finding fault with my behavior all day. Now she wanted me to let go of the card. Everybody was on my back about this card. Uncle Rollie, Big Stan, Charlotte . . . they had all turned against me. I couldn't remember the precise significance of the card, but I knew I was supposed to hold onto it and I could have used some support.

I was more hurt than mad. I saw Charlotte yelling at Mad Dog McClure and pointing at me. Then she got down on her hands and knees and screamed right in my face. I thought, this woman can't love me.

I looked down at the thing in my hand. The blurry face of an old-time ball player, unknown to me, looked back. Another of Dr. Frye's tests.

The worse you do in these intelligence tests, the more humiliated and embarrassed you are, the more comfort you take in physicality. The more stubborn and contrary you get. All right, very well then, I was a dummy. I couldn't remember what I held. I knew everybody wanted me to let go of it; I knew that much. So I wouldn't. Fuck 'em all, I decided. He died saying fuck 'em all.

Then I was coughing. The pressure around my neck had lessened, and lifted. I could get my fingers inside the lace. No, the lace was gone. I could breathe; I could cough.

I later learned that as Mad Dog McClure—who in my opinion would have made a fine World Wrestling Federation referee—had been about to pull Lee Vivyan off my insensible body, Vivyan had given a last good lethal yank, and the shoelace had snapped, as old shoelaces will. And the result of this was not only that I didn't pass out or die; it was that Lee Vivyan went into a severe decline.

As the blood and oxygen returned to my brain, and I slowly, hackingly worked my way back up to my feet, Vivyan remained on his knees, on the floor, staring at the laces in his hands. Now he had two.

He was devastated. He'd suddenly lost all his stuffing.

I can't say I knew the man well, but I think what Mad Dog said about him was right. Lee Vivyan had put all his faith in Hall of Famers. They were the foundation of his economic and emotional edifice, the only people he really counted on. And Joe DiMaggio was the cornerstone of this foundation. DiMaggio is not your run-of-the-mill Hall of Famer. He was considered, particularly in New York, the perfect ball player. He was the symbol of excellence and reliability, the stock that never went down.

So it wasn't just that Lee Vivyan had lost a treasured item in his inventory; it was the player that item represented. Lee Vivyan wasn't prepared for Joe DiMaggio's shoelace to break.

He just sat there while I got my breath back and stood up. My head felt inflated. I guess it was the rush of oxygen where oxygen was no longer expected. My neck felt skinned.

As normal vision returned, I found myself focusing on Lee Vivyan with a complete lack of sympathy. I was off him altogether. He'd robbed my uncle and tried to kill me. He'd been consistently rude all day.

Now he looked sad, lost, stunned. To me, all that meant was I finally had an opportunity to try something I'd picked up recently.

Charlotte, Uncle Rollie, and the rest of our group were standing around me. I put the card down on the empty table in front of Big Stan in order to prepare.

Then I bent over and ran head-on, full speed at Vivyan.

I got him on the rise. He'd apparently decided to blame me for the destruction of his showpiece, and was coming to his feet with a guttural roar when I caught him under the chin with the top of my head. He went ass over teakettle over a display table and I sprawled over the tabletop—for once, the butter instead of the buttee.

People were hollering. Somebody pounded me on the back. Mad Dog McClure worked his way between tables to check on Vivyan, who was flat on his back in a mess of memorabilia containers, with his head on a cardboard box, bicycling his legs. Mad Dog hunkered over him for a bit, then straightened up, walked over to me and lifted up my arm.

That was something.

Charlotte came up quickly on my right and hugged me, but before accepting any more congratulations, I wanted to get back to the card. As I started for the table where I'd left it, I happened to make eye contact with Billy Garner, who was standing beside Big Stan.

Billy's eyes widened. He hesitated. Then he grabbed the card and ran.

CHAPTER SEVENTEEN

Billy Garner had always been governed by impulse. According to Charlotte, the man was incapable of thinking ten feet ahead. The night before, after he'd left my apartment in the grasp of Big Stan, she'd told me about his coral business.

Shortly after Billy and his wife Brenda moved to LaPorte a few years ago, he disappeared for almost a month. Brenda didn't know where he'd gone. Nobody else knew or cared. He returned with a truck full of gray coral, which he'd bought in Florida and intended to bleach and sell at a huge profit all over the Midwest. The idea had evidently come to him while looking into an aquarium.

For several weeks, the Garner home and bathtub were filled with coral—gray, brittle, spiky branches. In order to shower, Brenda had to balance on the two ledges and duck.

The bleaching process was only marginally successful. And the market for gray coral in Missouri was sluggish. It's amazing, really, Charlotte told me, how few uses coral can be put to. The investment had ended up in about a trillion chunks in the Garners' backyard. Maybe someday the site will be a tiny archeological mystery.

Point of the story being that Billy Garner has a history of sudden inspiration, reckless behavior. Not too much reflection. But I can't really blame him for grabbing that Wildfire Schulte card. I can see why he did it.

I almost did the same thing when I saw his '59 Bob Gibson, back in Gordy O'Dell's tap. There's something about these cards that speaks to the kid in you, and the kid in you says, "Mine."

Billy'd been trying to get at it for a long time, and hadn't even been able to find it. This was the first time he'd ever seen it, much less been within grabbing distance; it all overcame him.

Security took out after him. So did Big Stan Cornell and several of the spectators. I couldn't do it; I was still too wobbly. Charlotte hollered, "Billy, you trash, I'm telling Brenda!" after him.

"They'll catch him," she assured me. "He won't even get off the floor."

He did, though.

He darted from one aisle to another, changed direction, doubled back and charged for the door. And he made it. It's true, in general, that when you stop drinking you can do things you couldn't do before.

But he couldn't get out of the building. Once in

the hallway, he found that security people were blocking all the street doors. I got to the Hall C entrance
in time to see him veering and careening back and
forth all over the corridor as people closed in on him
before and behind. Then he ducked into a stairwell.

Billy wound up looking down on all of us. He
ran upstairs and finally got chased by Security and
Big Stan out onto a limb—a grated iron light platform
overlooking one end of the card-show floor. He ran
to the end of the platform, where he came up against
the corner of the iron railing.

He had nowhere to go. But he had a hostage.

"I ain't givin' it back," he said to Big Stan, and
repeated it for all of us on the floor.

A Security man started walking toward him on
the platform, but stopped when Billy took the card
out of its sleeve and held it over the railing.

"I'll crumple it," he warned the guy. "I'll eat it."

"Give him room!" yelled Patterson at Security.
"He's got it out of the sleeve!"

"You're ruining a good start in AA, Billy," said
Big Stan.

"Back off," said Billy.

Big Stan looked down and found me.

"What should I do?" he asked me.

I ruminated.

"Well," I said, looking up at Billy, "don't run at
him."

"Billy," Charlotte called, "each thing you do is
more pitiful than the one before."

"You wanta stop raggin' on me, Charlotte?" he

hollered down at her. "You're all the time talkin' me down to Brenda."

"All right, I'll stop. She can just watch you slop your way through life."

"Let's don't antagonize him," I told her.

There were a couple new Merkel Security men on the floor. One of them was armed, and remarked to no one in particular, "I could probably drop him without hurting the card."

McCormick's head swiveled toward this young man, and he nudged Patterson.

Uncle Rollie was standing next to me, looking weary. I felt the same. We needn't have brought the card all the way up to Chicago for Billy to get it. We could've stayed in Missouri and left it on the doorstep.

Squinting up at Billy, who was whipping his head around defiantly at everybody and holding the card to his mouth, I felt helpless. I had never had much luck talking to him. I just rubbed him wrong. Maybe he thought I had had too many advantages in life.

"Think he might want to swap?" asked Uncle Rollie.

A man who can come up with an idea like that is not without mental resources. The rest of us had been standing there with our jaws hanging down. It took Roland Zerbs to produce the constructive thought.

I squeezed his shoulder and hurried off behind the clump of spectators clustered below the light platform until I reached Mad Dog and Diane McClure.

"This guy," I told them, "traded his Bob Gibson rookie card for beers down in LaPorte, Missouri, and he's never forgiven himself. Have you got a rookie Gibson I could buy?"

They both nodded, and Diane McClure said, "Come on."

"Billy, you wait!" I yelled. "Don't anybody rush him," I called up to Big Stan. "Just talk to him. Be nice. Encourage him. Say . . . AA things."

I followed her back to Mad Dog's booth, where she showed me a nice one in a hard plastic snap-on holder with a $200 tag on it.

"Very Good-Excellent," she said. "A little off-center but no corner wear. Couple little gum stains there . . . how about one-fifty?"

"That's nice of you."

She leaned forward and lowered her voice.

"When you sent Lee over the table, that was worth a discount. We all loved it. He's been crying *out* for that. It made the show for me; it was like a happy ending."

"Well, I'm afraid little Billy up there's got *our* happy ending, and he's getting beer sweat all over it."

"Oh, sorry," said Diane, handing me the card and my change.

I ran back under the light platform to serenade Billy.

He was still up there, holding the card, out of its sleeve.

"Billy, Billy. Put it down. Don't sweat on it."

"I'll *spit* on it if these guys don't back off."

219

"No, wait. Look. Look what I got here. See?"

He peered down at the snap-on I was holding up.

"It's the Gibson rookie. 1959. It's your old one. You give that thing back and it's yours, swear to God. Everybody here can hear me. I won't press charges, no hard feelings, no cops, you got it free and clear. Gibson, Billy. *Gibson.* Whaddya say?"

He looked down and said, "You're tryin' to gyp me."

I lost my temper and my conciliatory tone.

"Gyp you? *Gyp* you? You little shit, I'm trying to *help* you. There's people down here want to *shoot* you!"

Billy held the Schulte up in front of his face and hunched over.

McCormick and Patterson were still huddling with the young Merkel Security guard.

"Are you *sure* you can get him from here?" McCormick asked.

Charlotte turned on them.

"Now that's excessive. You just cut that talk out. There's been too much gun-waving around this whole thing. These are baseball cards. They don't even *sparkle*. They're supposed to be for kids. They aren't even worth Billy *Garner's* life."

McCormick was explaining to her how wrong she was, and Billy was calling down to me that he might consider a deal if I included a Lou Brock rookie, when we shut up, one by one.

Lee Vivyan had appeared on the platform.

*   *   *

Forgotten by all, bedraggled and bloody but risen again, he had left the floor and found the stairs. Now he stumped on past Big Stan and Security and advanced slowly across the grillwork like the great Karloff.

Billy didn't like the look on his face.

"You stay back," Billy said. "You watch out. I'll rip it. I'll tear it up."

Billy's feet were backing up, but he wasn't going anywhere, up against the corner of the platform.

Discarding the strategy he'd used in a similar situation with his old lady Pauline, Vivyan spent no time trying to convince Billy he loved him.

"Gimme," he said.

"Stop him!" Billy hollered.

Nobody did. Vivyan proceeded across the catwalk at a deliberate but even speed, his arms down, his fingers curled. I got the feeling that when he reached Billy he was going to tear pieces off him until he got to the card and then throw the remainder away.

In the end, Billy couldn't stand it. He didn't want to die. Big Stan later told me this is the key decision you have to make if you're ever going to have a chance at sobriety. Billy let out a little mini-shriek as Vivyan got within a few feet of him, and then made a convulsive kind of movement with his arm and flipped the card over the rail.

Wildfire Schulte, free for the first time in eighty-five years, fluttered side over side, high over our heads, toward the section of the floor being sudsed down and mopped by maintenance.

I was running in place. We all seemed to be. Nobody was getting anywhere. We were jostling frantically and hollering, and stepping on each other's ankles, but we had no chance. All we had was a view.

The old cards aren't thick cardboard; they're more like paper. They float, they flutter, they glide and dart, they ride the air currents. What they do, they head right to the wet part of the floor and the suds bucket.

A wet, soapy card is not a Near-Mint card and never will be.

People I didn't even know were in my way. By the time I got out of the clump it would be too late. And even if by some miracle I could get there in time to try to catch it, I knew I'd either miss it or crush it.

Lee Vivyan, up on the catwalk, bellowed in rage and despair and began shaking the insides out of Billy Garner. I don't know if I cried out, but I was no less agonized. All that work, all that hope, all that worry. All those lumps.

I felt Charlotte's fingernails digging into my forearm. She pointed, and I saw Dillon running.

He'd been on the periphery of the crowd, so no one was in his way. He was going full speed, intent and concentrated. Cutting across, like an outfielder, not going where the card *was,* but where he expected it to end up, over by the bucket.

He was moving well in his sneakers, like coordinated little kids do. He was the only one on the floor with a chance to get there. And he was the one person in the building, I'll bet, with recent leaf-catching experience. I screamed for him like a fan at a ball game. But I wasn't optimistic.

I'd seen him catch leaves. When Dillon caught leaves, he snatched them. Clutched them. And if he did that with the card, he might just as well miss it. I'd been at the show long enough to learn that crumpled cards don't feed the bulldog.

Now I'm not the baseball fan Mad Dog McClure is, and I'm sure Lee Vivyan would consider himself more knowledgeable than me. But I've seen some good ball players. When I was little I saw Curt Flood climb the centerfield wall at Busch Stadium. My cousin Charlie Tyke was a very good, underrated glove of the early '80s. I saw Ozzie Smith, many times, make plays that would force a gasp—a person and an object meeting when you didn't think a meeting possible. I've seen them all make leaping, diving stabs that barely failed, as well.

But I never had anything riding on any of those plays—which may be why the memory of Dillon's effort eclipses the others and burns through the haze, sharply defined.

The Schulte fluttered, paddle-wheeling backwards, then went into a faster downward glide toward the suds bucket. Dillon, farther away from the bucket but still going well, hit a patch of water and went into a feet-first slide, taking his Cardinals cap off with his right hand. The card dipped sharply. Dillon slid horizontally across the floor in front of the

223

bucket, his right arm extended, the cap held out as if he were begging. The card made a final, capricious swerve, and Dillon swiped at it.

He slid to a stop with his hand in the air, his cap in his hand, and the card in his cap.

We all took it pretty big. Charlotte was so delighted she knocked me five or six feet forward, and that gave me a start on everybody else who was running for Dillon.

I never saw a better catch, and I told him so when I got to him. With all those variables—the erratic movement of the card, the distance to cover, the slick floor, the necessity of catching it *gently* . . . it equaled any play I ever saw Curt or Ozzie or Cousin Charlie make. I caught myself looking for the replay on the overhead TVs.

Dillon was sitting on the wet floor when I skidded up to him. Charlotte was right behind me, and hugged him ferociously from her knees. He held the cap carefully, up and to the side. He had the shy smile of a kid who knows he's done good this time. It was one of those things you dream of doing—the great, crucial catch in front of everybody. His eyes glittered.

I lifted him up from behind, over my head, and put him on my shoulders to keep him and his cap above all the other people gathering around. Mad Dog McClure helped make a path for us to a nearby table.

On the way, I looked up to the catwalk. Big Stan was peeling Lee Vivyan off Billy Garner. I looked around for Carl but I couldn't see him.

When we reached the table, Dillon stepped onto it, off my shoulders. Charlotte brought Uncle Rollie over beside me, so we could all stand in front of him. Dillon fished carefully in his cap, took out the card, and handed it down to me. I took it between thumb and forefinger.

Wildfire was intact, not bent, but he had just the slightest bit of lumpiness at his lower corners. Residual moisture from Billy Garner's fingers.

I called up to Big Stan on the catwalk and asked him to look for the plastic sleeve.

"It's either on Billy or he dropped it," I told him.

"Never mind," said Mad Dog, coming forward. "You're in a room with a million of 'em. Here."

Back in a sleeve again, Wildfire looked his old self. I handed him to Uncle Rollie.

He took the card, gazed at it, turned it over and looked at the back, looked at the front again and, to my amazement, handed it back to me.

"You can hold it," he said.

I stared at him.

"Go on, Loren," he said, and patted me on the shoulder.

I held it up for all to see.

"The bidding," I announced, "is now open."

Up to this point, I'd allowed myself some private amusement in occasional speculation on how much we might get for Wildfire. My estimates had varied, depending on my mood, from five to twenty thousand dollars, always assuming we could find a lunatic.

225

I knew it wasn't enough that it was rare. I'm rare, but I'm not valuable, because I'm not in demand. No, people had to want it. In my more pessimistic moments I couldn't imagine why they would.

But then I had thought, why not? A baseball card has at least as much personality as a stamp, and collectors pay good money for old stamps. Too, this one was a picture of a Cub. Here we were in Chicago, where there are many Cub fans. And Cub fans . . . well, Uncle Rollie was right when he said it was like they had a disease. A fever. And one of the symptoms of fever is delirium.

So, in my sanguine moments I had entertained hopes of a decent offer. Uncle Rollie could live quietly in LaPorte for a long time on twenty thousand dollars.

But I hadn't taken Mad Dog McClure's remarks about big money as gospel, and I was a little thrown when the first bid we got, amid this mood of general jubilation, was "Forty thousand," from Mad Dog himself.

I looked at Diane McClure to see if she was going to drop a net over him, but she didn't even act surprised. I thought, Oh my.

I expected Uncle Rollie to be more flabbergasted than I was, but his brain protected him. He cocked his head to one side and asked cagily, "Forty thousand what?"

"Forty-five," said Nelson McCormick.

"Fifty," said Frank Patterson.

McCormick laughed. He shook his gleaming

head and grinned at Patterson.

"I'll tell you," he called to me, expansively. "I want to complete that set. I don't know any more about Frank Schulte than *he* does"—and he pointed at my uncle—"but I've got everybody else in that set—the whole lineup—and I'm gonna finish it to-night. I'll bid seventy to save time."

Uncle Rollie blinked at this point as if he'd suddenly wakened. He took the card from me and stared at it.

"Well, now, wait a minute," he said. "I *do* know about Frank Schulte."

He raised a hand, stopping the bidding. Then he looked at Dillon, who was behind us, leaning on his mother. Uncle Rollie gazed at Dillon as if he was seeing himself.

"My daddy had a meat market down on Cottage Grove for a while, you know," he said. "I used to sweep it out. Frank Schulte was his favorite. My daddy met him, told me all about him. They gave Schulte a car for the best player in the National League one year. A Chalmers. Cobb got one and Schulte got one. Wildfire was the name of his horse, did you know that? He raced a trotting horse in the wintertime. And this is curious, but Frank Schulte wrote poems in the newspaper, in Ring Lardner's column. My daddy read some to me."

Here Uncle Rollie struck a stance and looked upward and outward. Then he recited the following, with manly emotion:

227

"This base ball season soon will end
Or else I am a liar;
Then I'll go back to Syracuse
And drive my old Wildfire.
Against the fastest horses there
My old Wildfire will go
And show his heels to all of them
Upon the pure white snow.
How glad I am the time is nigh
When reins and whip I'll wield;
'Tis easier to drive a horse
Than run around right field."

His audience gradually went from mystification to restlessness during this performance. About six lines into it, Nelson McCormick looked as though he was being buried alive. Here he'd made one remark and in return he'd gotten Poetry Corner.

On one hand I was embarrassed for Uncle Rollie, feeling the sympathy pains you get when a loved one is dying onstage. On the other, I nearly applauded. I mean, here's a man on the lip of complete forgetfulness, tearing off a poem he couldn't have heard in the last fifty years—a poem no one else would remember for five minutes—and doing it without hesitation, keeping to the meter, even on that tricky "When reins and whip I'll wield" part. I should do so well with the "Gilligan's Island" song when I'm his age.

All the same, I had no idea where he was going with this recitation, and I didn't think he did either.

I was hoping he'd stop before he completely lost the house.

When he reached the end of the poem, he seemed to switch off to a siding momentarily, looking at the card again.

"I been having trouble," he said with perplexity and some sadness. "I can't seem to place a face, or stick to a plan. Either I leave the stove on too long, or I don't turn it on at all. I'll be wondering if I ate dinner and I'll go look in the little window and it's sitting there all frozen. Sometimes I think I'm losing my mind. You can't believe it."

He smiled slightly, raised his eyebrows, and sighed. Then he focused again.

"But when I look at this card I can see my daddy in his store, plain as that." He held up his index finger. "It *calls him up*. And I'm thinkin' now . . . I better not let it go. I don't have so many recollections that I can just sell one."

This drew a gasp from pretty much everybody. I know it got one from me.

Lee Vivyan, sitting bitterly up on the light platform with his legs hanging over the edge, called down, "Asshole's trying to jack up the price."

But I knew he wasn't. And everybody else got the idea when Uncle Rollie started walking toward the door.

I stood in a stupor for a moment, then ran after him and grabbed him by the arm.

"Hey. Hey. You can't do this. This is what we came up for."

"Well, I've changed my mind."

"Goddamn it, you don't *have*"—I changed direction—"you don't have any money. If you don't sell this card, we won't have anything to *put* in your stove. We're gonna be living on walnuts and snakes."

He wrenched his arm away from me.

"Loren," he said angrily, "I didn't mind Daddy givin' you money, because you needed it. You always need it. But he gave me this card to remember him by. To re*mem*ber him by. You silly sonofabitch."

He looked fiercely at me, then at the card again. Then he moved on.

As I stared after him I felt a tug on my arm, and Charlotte whispered urgently in my ear.

People who can think in a crisis are invaluable. Every family needs at least one such person.

I ran up to Rollie and whispered to him what she had whispered to me.

It stopped him. He looked at me, disbelieving. Then he reached in his shirt pocket and dug around.

"Well, goddamn," he said, pulling out the contents. "You're right."

He held both cards up, delighted.

"I got a *spare!*"

The sound of people bidding higher and higher for your uncle's baseball card is intoxicating. It's not precisely rhythmic, but you can move to it; I know this because Charlotte and I did. We swayed together while the numbers went up.

Uncle Rollie handled the role of auctioneer with

his old barkeeper's aplomb. You'd think he might have been overwhelmed by the spectacle of rich Chicago strangers fighting to throw him money, but he took it all in stride. Good fortune settled onto him like a soft floppy hat.

Mad Dog and Diane McClure came up to say good-bye when it got to $93,000.

"We're out," he said. "These guys have got it to burn."

"How about ten percent for setting it up?" I asked. "Would you consider that fair?"

The McClures looked at each other.

"There," said Diane. She turned to us. "I told him he'd miss something if he killed himself."

"That's acceptable, thank you," said Mad Dog, nodding gravely.

"He hasn't worked it through yet about . . . you know," said Diane. "He just needs to heal."

As the bidding between Patterson and McCormick built to a finish, Charlotte hauled a pad out of her bag and began sketching Uncle Rollie as auctioneer. Dillon lost interest, unable to relate the sums being thrown around to any familiar reality. He lay down on his back on the table and closed his eyes.

I took Mad Dog aside and got him to refer me to a guy on the show floor who had a copy of The Incredible Hulk #281—Wolverine's full debut. On the way up from Missouri Dillon had had nothing but good to say of Wolverine. As I went to make an offer for it, I looked up at the catwalk again.

Big Stan was talking earnestly to Billy Garner,

who was crumpled like a beanbag in the corner of the platform. Lee Vivyan was sitting with his legs hanging over the grating and his forehead on the middle iron rail. His eyes were closed. I could tell he was listening to the bidding, because his eyelids flickered and twitched in time with the increases.

I saw Carl, in the rear of a cluster of people on the floor. He gave what I took to be a sympathetic glance up at Lee Vivyan and then left the hall.

I made my deal and got back with Dillon's comic as Patterson finally won the card, pleasing Charlotte, who had taken a dislike to McCormick. The winning bid was $105,000.

Uncle Rollie closed the bidding with a ringing, resounding, "Going once, going twice, going, going, gone!"

Then he held up both cards for Patterson to see . . . the real one and the one Dee Francona made today.

"Which one you want?" he asked.

Patterson thought that was funny, but I think Uncle Rollie meant the question sincerely.

Charlotte was sitting on the table, finishing her sketch. She smiled and spoke before I could get started.

"Now you don't have to go back."

That caught me up short. I'd been adjusting my mind to returning to LaPorte to live. Now—she was right. I didn't have to.

"What are *you* gonna do?" I asked.

She blinked, mildly surprised at the question, and continued sketching.

"Go home. Dillon's got school. I took him out two days for this trip. And I need to get back to work. I don't believe Mr. Green Genes is going to cushion me for life."

In her drawing, Uncle Rollie was pointing authoritatively outward, a man in control of his destiny, a man with his eyes clear, his hand steady, and his fly open. I looked up at the model and waved to get his attention. He interpreted my pantomime correctly, adjusting himself while talking to Patterson.

Charlotte glanced critically at my bruises and bumps as I sat back beside her.

"You look," she told me, "as though you dove into an empty swimming pool and then hanged yourself."

"You don't find that look attractive?"

"Well, I'll say it took some nerve," she said, "holding onto the card through that. That's the Cooper I remember."

I summoned up my leftover bravery.

"Speaking of remembering . . . you know my memory's spotty. I was thinking, I don't want to take a chance on forgetting you, and I thought if . . . we were to get together, I wouldn't have to worry. I mean . . . there you'd be."

Her eyebrows raised. She fanned herself.

"Burning words, Cooper."

I nodded, shamefaced.

"I know. Not so good. I should've written it

down and then gone over it."

She held up her finished sketch. The signature read "Charlotte Prine."

"If I understand what you're sneaking up on here, Cooper," she said, "I just recently got back to myself. See? Prine?"

"I think Prine is fine. I don't have any problem with that."

She looked at me doubtfully.

"Well, then, what are you talking about? Something serious? Or just a hot little high school reunion?"

"How about first the one and then the other?"

She laughed.

"Well, you know I'm going home."

We sat against the table in silence for a moment, watching the remaining dealers pack up.

I thought, I don't know why everybody should be going home except me.

CHAPTER EIGHTEEN

It's Indian summer in LaPorte. No humidity, flooding, thunderstorms, or tornadoes. Just clear air, temperate breeze, and sun on the water.

Today was the second day after the Chicago auction. Word got around town quickly about Uncle Rollie's big score; down in Gordy O'Dell's cellar they think he got a half million.

We came back yesterday, without Billy Garner, who is staying up in Chicago until next Thursday in order to attend a full week of meetings with Big Stan Cornell.

We were on the riverbank this afternoon—Charlotte, Dillon, Mom, and me—standing on the cement foundation which is all that's left of Thorpe's boathouse. Uncle Rollie was home sleeping.

Charlotte had completed a penciled rendering of what the new boathouse should look like, and she was showing it to me and Mom. Dillon was over on the remains of Thorpe's pier, sidearming stones into the river.

The drawing was impressive. It showed the building on pillars, to stand above normal flood level, and a rebuilt pier with gas pumps on it, riding the river in front. There were huge windows facing the water, and a large sign across the top under the roof gutter, saying "Rollie's Jr."

I liked it. Mom thought it was too dependent on a weak reed.

"Roland Zerbs," she declared, "is incapable of presiding over a family meal, much less a family restaurant. I don't care how much money he got for that card. The fact that you found someone in Chicago who's more impaired than he is doesn't alter his condition." She looked at me. "He thinks you're his brother. He calls you Loren half the time."

I shrugged.

"He'll do all right. He wants to do it. He's got money to get it started, and Charlotte's the brains."

Mom snorted. "And what are you?"

"He's the dumb nerve," said Charlotte.

"You know," I told Mom, "I've been feeling better ever since I butted that guy in the head in Chicago. It seemed to relieve the pressure."

"That's not what you told *me* relieved the pressure," Charlotte muttered.

Lloyd Wiemeier's car scrunched up on gravel and parked beside Charlotte's, facing the river. Lloyd got out and greeted Dillon.

"Next weekend," he said.

" 'Kay, Dad."

Lloyd walked up to us and talked while looking out toward Illinois.

"Hear you two are gonna build this thing back up," he said.

"That's right," said Charlotte.

"Good for you. Good for the town. Your uncle's got curiosity value, might bring in some gawkers." He squinted at me. "I knew you'd move in on her."

"Guess that's why you get the big money, Lloyd," I said.

"You got your first visitor already," he went on. "Fella drove in and stopped at the 76 and asked for Rollie's house. Jimmy Poe talked to him. Reporter, he said."

"Yeah?"

"Jimmy thought he might be one of these boys works for the *Enquirer* or one of them. Said he had a cast on his arm and a poor disposition."

I got a spasmodic chill.

"Mustache?" I asked.

"I don't know," said Lloyd.

"Did Jimmy tell him where to go?"

"Well, he told him where Rollie lives."

I started running toward Charlotte's car.

We heard one gunshot and knew right away where it came from.

I drove Charlotte's car. Everybody else followed as they could, in Belle's car or Lloyd's, I don't know.

I spun onto Front Street and went through the

light and two signs until I got to the gravel road past the grain silo. I went up that road in a cloud of dust and skidded to a stop behind a dirty Ford Taurus in Uncle Rollie's driveway.

Lee Vivyan was wriggling on his back in the drive, his gun a few feet away. He did indeed have a cast on his left forearm.

Wendell Kendall stood at the top of the steps of his mobile home, going through the manual of arms with his shotgun as he tried to get past the screen door.

I walked over to Lee Vivyan's gun and picked it up. It looked as though Wendell had shot him in the left buttock.

"He thought you were from the Fairfax Gypsum plant," I told him.

"Oh, shit, go on, finish me off," said Vivyan through gritted teeth. "I'm a fuckin' horse with a broken leg, I'm going into shock here."

Uncle Rollie was outside now, too, hobbling slowly toward us from the house. His hair was pointing everywhere and his fly was open again, but it was excusable under the circumstances. Cars came up behind me. Uncle Rollie reached us and looked down at Vivyan.

"Who the hell is this?" he asked.

Uncle Rollie sat in the folding chair on the end of his pier. I stood beside him. Behind us and up the bank, there was a sizable crowd, for LaPorte. State police from Canton and everybody from downtown. Gordy O'Dell and several guys from the tap. Charlotte, Dillon, Mom, Wendell. Even Callie McAllister from Quincy, Uncle Rollie's girlfriend, who had come to visit in her Buick. She must have missed him while he was gone.

The old man and I looked across at the trees on the Illinois side. It was late afternoon now. The river rolled by, lazy and polite.

Uncle Rollie had combed his hair, but only after I'd started to do it for him myself. He was zipped up and presentable. But he wasn't sharp, no getting around it. He'd responded very vaguely to everyone up in his yard. He wasn't too sure who anybody was. I was trying to bring him up-to-date.

"You know we were just up in Chicago," I said.

"Uh-huh, I know that."

"You know why?"

He grunted.

"I don't have time to worry about that."

"One of the guys from up there came to rob you today, or shoot you. Wendell got him, though."

Uncle Rollie's head snapped back with astonishment.

"*Shoot* me? Bullshit. What for?"

"We beat him out for some money."

"I don't have any money."

"Well, you do. You've got enough money to open the boathouse and call it Rollie's Jr."

He laughed, genuinely tickled.

"You're a touch. You're a caper. You're a dancin' fool, Loren. I don't know what to do with you."

I was worried. He didn't sound good. I didn't

want him to float away from me. I needed to light some spark of recall in him.

"Don't you remember the card show? Don't you remember that I'm Cooper?"

His eyes widened. Then he squeezed them shut, embarrassed and angry with himself.

"God, I didn't." He opened his eyes and looked across the river, then sighed and spoke shakily. "You can't believe it."

He'd lost all we'd done in the last two days, and I couldn't think of anything to say to bring it back for him. We were silent for the time it took the current to carry a tree branch past us. Finally, I grasped at one last straw.

"Don't you even remember Misty Rue and Her Twin Bazookas?"

He was immobile for a moment.

"I sure don't," he said at last. Then he glanced back up the bank at Charlotte. "And you'd better not, either."

A key came down on the page in the fish typewriter below us, and I jumped, as usual. The fish were still hard at work.

"How they doin'?" I asked him.

"Ohh, they're stealin' now," he said wearily.

"What?"

He bent over with a grunt, and rolled the page up a bit. Then he cleared his throat, and read to me.

" 'Fond memory brings the light of other days around me.' "

Then he straightened up.

"If they didn't steal that I'll eat this pier."

He rose, turned, and stumped back up the bank, and I stayed, looking down at the river.

AFTERWORD

According to *Bartlett's,* the sentiment in Uncle Rollie's fish typewriter was indeed lifted, from the poet Thomas Moore (1779–1852). It appeared in the first stanza of a little thing of his called "Oft in the Stilly Night." One of the Quincy TV stations sent a woman out two days later to tape a report on the phenomenon—on the lighter side. Most of the fingers in LaPorte are pointing not at the fish, but at Jerome Tunney, an antique dealer and joker who once stuck half his inventory in the woods west of town to convince people there was an undiscovered Amish settlement hidden there. The opinion at Gordy O'Dell's tavern is that Jerome sneaked out on the pier while we were gone and tapped out the quotation. He denies it, laughing.

I'll say this: Jerome may have finished that line, but I personally know the fish started it.

Uncle Rollie disowned the line on the Quincy

telecast, declaring he was completely versus plagiarism no matter by whom. He took the opportunity to read a couple authentic oldies from his collection.

His performance was picked up by some other stations and resulted in a phone call from an editor in Colorado whose publishing house—Purple Cow Press—specializes in experimental and multicultural poetry. The editor said he'd been impressed by the echoes of e. e. cummings in the second poem Uncle Rollie read:

delta mire in
holy toes
was no clod garbo
late boy

"Late Boy" has always been a favorite of Uncle Rollie's, too. He reads it as a guy kicking himself for letting love elude him. Aside from its poignance, he says it's the longest the fish ever stuck to one subject.

This editor says Purple Cow is willing to offer a small cash advance for a paperback printing of the collected works "once the question of authorship is resolved."

Of course we're all proud of Uncle Rollie and his fish, and I'm in disgrace for ignoring their potential all these years. I'm glad he's unable to dwell on it.

Charlotte recently heard a radio psychologist discussing men who make love to women until they marry them, and then can't. We've decided that my first big test in this area will come on the evening of January 8th. Uncle Rollie has agreed to be my best man, and Dillon has agreed to be my stepson.

Charlotte will retain her professional name of Prine, Dillon is still a Wiemeier, and I'm not changing from Zerbs, so everybody in the new family will have their own name, like states in the union, we hope.

I'm staying with Uncle Rollie right now. We're buying groceries with the last of my Neatly Chiseled money as we forge ahead toward our new career as restaurateurs. Uncle Rollie looks forward to the opening of his new establishment, and has recovered physically from our trip. Mentally, he's about the same so far. I'm happy about this, since change is unlikely to be for the better.

Wendell Kendall is still next door, having been quickly exonerated of wrongdoing in the shooting of Lee Vivyan. Wendell seems less troubled now. They finally came and he got 'em, is the way he looks at it.

We've hired a retired nurse named Amy Ritt to come in three times a week and fight the clutter in Uncle Rollie's house. She says the place is a mountain of junk, and she's right. We've thrown some of this Zerbsiana out, but not as much as Amy wants us to. Uncle Rollie and I have acquired a keen appreciation for junk; you attach extra value to the past if you've ever lost access to it. Uncle Rollie still floats out beyond gravity quite often, and needs his mementoes to keep him tethered to the ship.

I have some mementoes of my own. In the closet upstairs there's a box of comic proofs, old memos, and scraps from Neatly Chiseled Features. I consult it when I forget what I did for those years.

But my favorite Chicago keepsakes come from the end of my stay there:

Item One is a Very Good-Excellent 1959 Bob Gibson card that Billy Garner claims rightfully belongs to him. I haven't gotten to where I agree with him yet.

Two through Five are four photographs showing Uncle Rollie, Dillon, the Wildfire Schulte card, Charlotte, and me at the Michigan Avenue bridge. They're nice clean photos, with no creases or corner wear.

Last is an original Charlotte Prine sketch of my uncle presiding over a big-time card auction, looking much as he did when he watched his customers roll their hoops down Front Street thirty years earlier.

These items are presently on the second shelf of the bookcase in the sitting room. Now and then they catch my eye, and fond memory brings the light of other days around them.

AUTHOR'S NOTE

The Frank Schulte poem recited by Rollie Zerbs appeared in Ring Lardner's column in the *Sporting News* in December, 1910.

The likelihood is that the poem was written by Lardner himself, according to Jonathan Yardley's biography *Ring* (1977, Random House).